Off Limits

Book II in the Nitty Gritty series

By Renee Pace

Acknowledgments

Thanks always to my loving husband Brian and my children for understanding my need to write. To all the teens out there with secrets they are afraid to reveal remember you are not alone. Ever.

Chapter 1

Lindsay

"You coming over tonight, Rebecca?"

I make the question casual, like it's no sweat off my back if my best friend can't come over tonight. Inside my gut twists and rolls with the thought of being alone. She plays with her dyed blonde ponytail, pulling the strands tight to her head to fluff it up higher. She's not paying attention to me. Rebecca's one focus is Blair. Blair's main focus is Rebecca. They make me sick.

"Can't Linds. I've got plans."

I hate that nickname and no matter how many times I ask her not to call me that she doesn't listen. She dismisses me with a swish of her ponytail and walks over to plant one on Blair's lips. I cringe with disgust. For the life of me I can't understand what she sees in him, besides his muscular body. Muscle or not, he's not something I'm into.

I re-read the text from my mother and resist the urge to type a pleading note back to her not to spend another night away. Mom's been at a conference all weekend. I had Friday, Saturday and even Sunday night covered. It's Monday. She was supposed to come home tonight. Now I'm left scrambling for an excuse to spend the night somewhere else or begging a friend to come to my house for a sleepover. Worse, I have to make my impromptu sleepover sound casual, like it's an afterthought that me, the so-called perfect girl in this Prep school, wants a friend or better yet friends to spend Monday night at her house. No one has sleepovers on Monday. Even I know that. Thing is, I'm all into bucking the trend. Especially when a friend will keep me safe and they won't even know it.

Taking the time to look at my reflection staring back at me thanks to my handy-dandy locker mirror I reapply my pink lipstick, add a bit more black eyeliner around my bottom lids and flick my long blonde hair off my shoulders. I look cool and sophisticated thanks to Mother's recent shopping spree and my practiced 'I'm fine' look. I'm totally decked out in designer duds, from my shoes to my new hot purple matching bra and underwear, although no one's going to see *that.* It's the top of the line on this bod. But just once I wish I didn't feel like trash. They say clothes make the woman. My clothes, like the makeup I carefully apply, are my body armor. They protect me and conceal me. Even my scars—carefully hidden thanks to my long-sleeved sweater. They are my shame. My dirty little secret I can't tell anyone.

Armed with my new Coach purse, another gift from Mother-dearest, I saunter to class. It would not be cool for me to be late so I never am. Appearances must be maintained and just like my good grades, which are totally expected, I play my part to a T.

The class is totally boring and I can't absorb one freaking word the teacher is droning on about. Something to do with DNA, mitochondria and cellular fusion. I hate biology. You of course would never know that. My last test was a ninety-eight percent and I participate in class even though inside it kills me.

"Mr. Turner, I didn't catch the last part of what you were saying, do you mind repeating it?" I make sure to bat my eyelashes at him and throw in a flirty smile. Sometimes using the way I look makes me sick. Not today.

"Sure Lindsay, as I was saying..."

This time I take notes. It helps me concentrate on his class, forcing my mind not to wander into that dark place. An itch starts on both of my wrists but I don't scratch. Scratching would ruin the plastic surgeon's work and piss my mother off to no end. My mother and I don't talk about the "incident". That's her word, not mine. I have another word I like to use, but uttering that makes her angry. Trust me, that's not pretty.

We went from Halifax, Nova Scotia to Mexico, just the two of us, but not once did we talk about anything important. The five and a half hour flight might have never happened. But it did. The "incident" happened and now...now, I am supposedly all better. *As if!* And like all mistakes, we wiped all memories of it clean from our lives. Well, that's how Mother viewed it. Me, I'm not so sure.

Now we live in Toronto. To say I hate this place would be an understatement. Gone is my tree. The one tree that grew up wit me. Mother planted it in our backyard, blubbering away about "us" making our own memories when my father walked out on us. She never once looked back at that relationship, except to look at me. I should have been the wise one. Make one stupid mistake Lindsay and voilà, you'll get taken away from all you know, including the stupid silly things that shouldn't matter, but do. Like that tree, which had been on a piece of property in my mother's family for close to two hundred years. She sold off the acreage to some developer, but not before we trekked an hour back into the bug-infested woods for that damn shrub. Cedar. That's it. We didn't think it would survive but that tree did. It grew and grew, so much so, that it became my own special tree. Now, that's gone. After all the shit that's happened in my life, I honestly can't believe I miss that stupid tree.

My mother couldn't live with the shame of my so-called accident. The reality is she couldn't live with the gossip and still to this day, a full six months later, she is not interested in learning the truth. I tried to tell her it wasn't an accident. That didn't go so well.

"What did he say?"

Without turning my head I answer Megan. She's sitting next to me, only because she got assigned that seat. Megan, with her mousy-brown hair, is about as boring as you can get. The cosmetic ladies would have a field day with her face. I bet she doesn't even own lip gloss. I look at her for a good twenty seconds.

Beggars can't be choosers.

"You doing anything tonight?" I turn my head slightly, giving her a bit of my attention but not all of it. Inside my head I am still going through all my friends, trying to figure out who might say yes to coming to my house tonight. Most of my friends have cheerleading practice on Monday night. Since I couldn't even try out for the team because of my "weak" wrists lie, I'm not on it. Neither is Megan.

She hasn't answered me, so I'm forced to look at her. "Megan, you busy tonight?"

She gives me a puzzled expression. "No. Why?"

"Want to come over?"

"Over. Like, as in to your house to do homework or something?" I can't help notice how her uni-brow furrows in frustration and she's got a pack of whiteheads on her nose that could seriously use some medication. What she really needs is a good makeover. Oh. My. God. I am a genius.

I move my chair slightly closer to her. "Look, come to my

house tonight and we'll give each other makeovers."

Her eyes widened and honestly the biggest smile on the planet lights up her face. I feel like a heel. What the hell am I thinking? Oh, I know; I'm not thinking. I'm desperate. I can't believe Megan is my last hope.

"Sure. That would be great. I can come over for a bit."

A bit. I need her to commit for the night. "I was thinking…you know, there's nothing going on…why don't you spend the night?" I gulp. It's too late to swallow back the words but I know I have just committed social suicide. For a second I wonder which is worse—home alone or having Megan over.

"A sleepover?"

Thank god she asks the question in her whisper-like voice. "Yeah," I nod. "A sleepover, that's a great idea." *I am so royally screwed.* I made her think sleeping over at my house was her idea. It's not, but if it will get her to commit, I don't care what she thinks.

"You sure?" she asks.

Not really, but I don't have anyone else to ask and you're my last hope. I nod, making sure my smile is bright and full, stretched taut across my face. I notice she's still taking notes. How the hell can she concentrate on this boring stuff when my guts feel like they are being twisted into pretzel shapes?

"Just you and me, tonight at my house for a makeover. Come around six and we'll have time for a movie later."

"You sure your parents won't mind? It being Monday night and all."

"My mother's away at some stupid work conference. And my stepfather doesn't care what I do." And that's the truth. He only cares about one thing but that's not going to happen—if she comes over, that is.

"You are so lucky. By the way, I don't have any makeup to bring."

"Don't you worry. I have enough stuff to outfit my own store. When I'm done with you tonight you can take whatever you want home with you."

"I wish I had your life."

I gulp. A flash of terror slides through my skin at her words. If she knew my real life, if she knew what went on in the dark, when

Mother's not home, she most certainly would not want my life. I can't say anything for a full minute. Instead, I start to take notes again. My heart's hammering away and sweat glides down my new shirt. I'm glad now I put on my sweater.

"You okay?" she asks.

"You bet. Just plotting out in my head what we're going to do tonight."

The bell rings. Class is over. I gently close my laptop. No one carries scribblers or school books at this school. It's high-tech all the way. The sickening part is that with it being mid-morning, religious class is next. I am not one bit Catholic, even though my mother said we were. I fake my way through religious class much like how I pretend being happy. Guess I learned how to lie from a pro. The worse part about my next class is with it being Monday it's mandatory confessional. Honestly, some of my best lies take place in the privacy of a wooden closet. Just me and the priest, separated by a silly wooden barrier. I should journal some of the "indecent" things I confess. They sound exciting even to me so, I can just imagine the hard-on they give that fat, disgusting priest. If there's one thing I have learned in the past year it's how to spot a pervert. Trust me, he's just like Greg, my stepfather, who ever since I turned fourteen has snuck into my room to show me his idea of loving. The concept of *that* type of love is not something I want. If that's loving, I will take hate any day.

I know something the priest and most of my fellow students don't know. There is no hell in the afterlife. I've been there. Died for a good three minutes. I didn't feel a thing. Only this life is living hell.

"See you at six," I remind Megan, as we casually join the mass exit from class.

"Can't wait," she says.

I can't help noticing the bounce in her step. It should make me happy. It doesn't. I don't even like Megan. She's a pathetic excuse for protection but she will have to do.

Chapter 2

Megan

I'm doing time calculations in my head. There is no way I can make it home, which takes me a good hour and get back in time to meet Lindsay at six. Shit! What the hell was I thinking? Oh, I know I was thinking maybe someone wanted to really be my friend at this school.

Moving away from the school, I wait until it's totally clear before calling home. No sense getting caught. Using the one public phone about four blocks away, I drop my quarter in and dial, praying no one I know walks by. It's so not cool to not own a cellphone but like Mom points out, "It's not the end of the world." Maybe not to her, but for me, it makes me a social pariah.

"Mom, is it okay if I stay at Lindsay's house tonight?" I tell her about a huge assignment we so don't have but these days if lying will make my life easier, I do it. She asks me a bunch of other questions and even threatens to drop off my clothes. *Like that's going to happen.* Mom's been in a wheelchair for the past decade because of MS and the thought of her attempting to make her way to one of the accessible subway lines makes me shiver.

"Seriously, Mom, stop being so over-protective. All is good. Lindsay says I can borrow some of her clothes. *Wouldn't that be cool and amazing.* It's no worry and not a bother. I'll give you a call…what, what…I can't hear you. The line's getting fuzzy. Don't worry. I'll call you in the morning, okay? Love you." I hang up before she asks once again to talk to one of Lindsay's parents. Like I'd ever let that happen. No way!

I officially have a good hour to kill before I walk to Lindsay's house. I know exactly where she lives. Everyone in the school does. She lives in the mega-mansion at the end of the cul de sac about two blocks from the school. Must be nice to only have to get up ten minutes before class and not worry about being late. For a second I let that jealous feeling harden, like a peach pit in my stomach. Then I remember the expression on Lindsay's face when she asked me to her house. It wasn't a look normally plastered to her polished façade.

Slowly making my way to the city's library I pass four coffee houses. I'm dying for a cup but yesterday I calculated how much money I've been spending on java and figured the money I save by not buying will go to a better use. My mom's been saving for two years now. She needs at least twenty thousand to cover all her expenses for the MS liberation procedure. At the end of this year, with my no-coffee-buying money I can contribute over four hundred. With my part-time army reserve job I can add another three thousand. It's not a lot but every penny counts. That's her motto and me and my older brother live by that. Or, we used to.

I try hard not to think about him. My skin starts to get clammy and for a second I think I'm going to puke. Right there on the sidewalk with all these rich kids walking past me like I'm dog shit. Forcing my gag reflex to stop, I get a grip on my emotions.

I straighten trying not to slouch as I walk through the library doors. Someone's added more graffiti to the gray concrete side wall. I flash a smile at one of the librarians, and head to my usual haunt. Up two flights of stairs, take a left and you enter the world of specialized literature. It's my favorite part of the library. The books are all hard cover and bible-thick. Some are written in foreign languages, but most are in Latin or old English. If the kids at school found out that in my spare time I like to study Latin I would be a laughingstock. Wait a sec, I'm already that. Hunkering down in the only chair in this part of the library, I make sure the coast is clear before I haul out my thermos. Time for my own homemade brew. It's a little cold, after suffering a day in my small locker, but I'm not about to pass up a much-needed jolt of caffeine. I check twice to make sure no one is around and then fish out my sandwich.

Removing my sweater, I think about what I can say to Lindsay. Not a lot comes to mind. We are night and day. She's rich, spoiled and *Cosmo* beautiful. Everyone loves her. Me. I'm a nobody. The only reason I'm at the private school is thanks to a scholarship I got through some help from my reserve commander who says he sees real potential in me. He sees potential in lots of people but even I was floored when he offered to write a reference to the school on my behalf. If my so-called school friends, none of which I really have, knew I was there at the Prep school only because of my scholarship, or if they had an inkling of where I hail from, well I might as well get lice. Seriously, I would be the biggest social outcast and I am not going to let that happen. This school is my stepping stone for getting into a university. Nothing and no one is going to squash my dream. My mom's counting on me. And that's why my mouth is shut. That's why my identity in school has to remain hidden.

I realize I've been moping about my life way too long. Checking the time on the large old-fashioned round clock mounted high on the wall, I repack a piece of my sandwich, which as usual, I didn't dare open or unwrap in school. Tucking my thermos back inside my bag, I get up and stretch. Why did I say yes to Lindsay? Now, I'm going to have to wear my clothes twice in a row, which is so beyond uncool I'm thinking of cancelling and going home. But home isn't home anymore, and I never get asked by anyone to spend the night with them.

I make my way out of the library and head toward her house. My stomach's feeling sort of queasy. Maybe cold coffee wasn't such a great idea. I step up to Lindsay's house and I'm about to knock on the large mahogany door when it startles me by opening.

"Took you long enough. I was getting worried."

She actually looks like she was. She opens the door wider and I enter into a world so beyond my two-bedroom apartment I almost make a dash for the exit. Her hand grabs my arm.

"Lindsay, is there someone here?" A loud booming male voice invades the space as I allow Lindsay to haul me inside the large, airy foyer.

"Yeah, there is. My *friend* Megan's spending the night, Greg. That's my step-father."

She whispers the last part like I hadn't figured that out. I'm not stupid. Proof in point the twenty thousand dollar scholarship I got to go to school. What I can't figure out is if Lindsay meant what she said. Am I really her friend? Or by her panicked expression, am I just the body she needed tonight so she didn't have to be alone with her step-dad? The fact I understand her body language raises the hairs on the back of my neck.

Chapter 3

Lindsay

I thought for sure Megan was going to be a no-show. I can tell by her startled look, with those piercing green eyes of hers, she's wondering why I'm acting like I am. Well, if you had to worry about being alone with Greg, you'd act like a freak too. Forcing myself to get a grip, I watch her take it all in. I can just imagine what she's thinking. Spoiled rich kid. She's got part of that correct. Spoiled. Check one. Rich. Check two. Kid. Not so much. I stopped being a kid the moment Greg snuck into my bedroom over two years ago. Kids cry. A kid runs and tells their mommy they're hurt and their mommy makes them all better. Not my mother.

"This place is amazing," she says. "So where's your room?"

She's acting so nonchalant I don't buy it. Again, I'm wondering if I've made the biggest mistake of my life. Then I hear Greg moving around in the kitchen. He's looking for the beer I hid. Last time I did that, he flipped out on me. Again, Mother dearest wasn't around. I pleaded ignorant but when he found the liquor a few days later, he poured a can all over me, ruining my shirt. His only joke was I should enter a wet-T shirt contest. I didn't bother responding. He's such a fucking prick! I did the only thing I could. I marched into my room, locked the door to the washroom—that's the only room with a lock—and took a shower. Then I threw out my clothes. I didn't mention the incident to my mother. Why bother? He'd twist it into something gross and disgusting and make her hate me more than she already does.

"My room's upstairs. Where's your bag?"

The minute I ask I see panic flash across Megan's face. Oh shit, if she's thinking of leaving I will seriously lose it.

"Don't worry if you forgot it. I've got lots of clothes. You can borrow anything you want."

She follows me upstairs and says, "Are you serious?"

We're almost at the top when Greg saunters out of the kitchen, shirtless and all. I resist the urge to flee with Megan but I'm hoping she won't notice.

"Hi. You must be Lindsay's friend," says Greg, walking up the freaking stairs like it's normal to walk around half-dressed.

"Nice to meet you," says Greg.

He's a step below Megan and holding out his hand for her to shake. I feel sick. Normal fathers do not walk around half naked. He's flexing his chest muscles for Megan and I can't resist rolling my eyes at him. Of course he notices and flashes me one of his sexy smiles. I don't think they're sexy, but he does. If a shark can smile and look harmless that's exactly how Greg looks when he flashes his pearly whites. They are only pearly white because of all the enhanced cosmetic attention his teeth, face and tanned body receive thanks to my generous Mother. She likes to throw out the comment to anyone listening, he's her boy-toy and really only good for one thing. Thinking of that one thing makes me want to puke.

"Nice to meet you Greg. I'm Megan."

"Lindsay's never mentioned you before."

He's goading her on to annoy and embarrass me. I flash a smile at Megan but it's hard to do since I'm a step ahead of her on the stairs. She turns her head and smiles at me, but the smile doesn't reach her eyes. Funny how I notice that.

"That's okay. We sort of just became friends, didn't we Lindsay," she says.

I nod, feeling robotic with my movements. "Yeah, we did. Anyway, Megan and I are busy tonight Greg. We're doing girly things."

He laughs. I notice Megan doesn't.

"Well, trust me I don't want to get in the way of girly things. I'm about to order pizza. You girls want some?"

"Sure that would be nice," says Megan, before I can tell Greg to fuck off and leave us alone.

He nods. "The usual Linds."

When Greg calls me Linds I almost hurl right there on the steps. He's such a waste of a human being. I manage a curt nod and then race up the rest of the stairs. Only when I hear Megan's echoing footsteps does it dawn on me I'm being rude.

I flop down on my bed. She stands in the middle of my room. Her eyes aren't looking at my room though. She's looking right at me, like she can see me with all my scars and it scares me shitless.

"Should I have told your step-dad I'm a vegan?"

"What?" I say.

She laughs, the sound startling soft. "I was kidding, Lindsay. Just kidding."

I'm so happy she didn't call me Linds I sit up and smile. A real, thank you smile, letting the tension ease from my body.

"So what's your usual?"

She's still talking about the stupid pizza. "The works, loaded with onions." I give a nervous laugh. She doesn't understand that onions make me reek, and just like garlic for warding off vampires, onions ward off Greg.

"Sounds delicious."

"Oh, it is." For the first time all day, I think this night might be okay.

Chapter 4

Megan

My face is so loaded with makeup I don't even recognize myself.

"See, I am a genius." Lindsay turns my head back to the bathroom mirror. I can't help but gawk. I look totally different—almost pretty.

She's right. She's an artist when it comes to my face. I keep blinking. I think there is too much mascara on my eyelashes. I swear to god I had a dozen zits on my nose this morning when I woke up. After she made me put on a smelly mud facial wrap they got peeled off. My uni-brow, after all that painful plucking, is also gone.

"I might have overdone it a tad with the mascara."

Her head is so close to mine as she peers into the large mirror I can smell the lilac perfume she sprayed on her neck. I would have loved the perfume but I worry any scent will set off one of Mom's wicked headaches, so I politely decline her generous offer.

"No. It's all great." And it is. The outline of the dark green eyeliner makes my eyes look like they are neon green.

"Makeup makes you look a lot older," says Lindsay. "Now I know why your parents don't let you wear it."

I turn my head to look at her. She's outlined her eyes in heavy black eyeliner, giving her a sexy Goth look. It makes her look like she's twenty or something instead of sixteen and it doesn't suit her. "I don't think your mom would like the Goth look."

"Oh my god she totally hates it. I usually only wear it when she's not around. I wouldn't get a foot out the door if she caught me looking like this and trust me a lecture from her is not worth the makeup."

She starts removing the makeup with a delicate makeup remover. I didn't even know there was such a thing.

"So, what's with your parents anyway…all teens wear makeup. It's no biggie," she says.

I resist the urge to tell her I don't have parents, only my mom, and half the time her meds knock her out so she's not someone I can count on. Not that I blame her one bit. Between her headaches and constant joint pains, I'm sure I'd pop pills for relief.

"My mom's like super-sensitive to scented products. I even have to use no-scent deodorant," I say, hoping she'll drop it.

"Oh my god, I heard of people like that. You know what, let's go to the drug store right now and buy some no-scented makeup."

Shit. This isn't what I want to do at all. First off, I don't have any money for makeup and second, even if I did have money I don't want to spend it on lip gloss, eyeliner and other stuff that will only make me feel guilty whenever I use it.

"Scratch that idea. Let's go pop up popcorn and watch Scream II," she says, letting me breathe easy for a moment.

In the course of three hours I have discovered Lindsay likes to bounce from one thing to another. It's like she's not comfortable in her own skin or in her own house.

"Now that sounds like a plan." I plop down off the bathroom counter and follow her back into her bedroom.

"You girls having fun?" asks Greg.

I wonder how long he's been standing quietly inside Lindsay's bedroom. The guy creeps me out. By the sheer look of terror on Lindsay's face the feeling is mutual. Her entire body has gone from relaxed to as stiff as gobs of mascara on my eyelashes. She's fisted her hands together by bunching up the material on the long baggy sweater she's wearing. The sweater is ugly and not at all what I thought she would ever wear in public. Then again, we're not exactly in public.

"Yeah, loads of fun," I say, because Lindsay's not speaking.

"Get out of my room, Greg."

Lindsay doesn't move a muscle. She's speaking through her teeth and staring at him with a look most people at our school could easily decipher. Loosely translated, her expression says 'fuck you! You're dog shit and not worth my time of day'. I know that look. She's used it on me more than once. Again, I wonder what I'm really doing here.

"Don't use that tone with me, young girl," says Greg

"Get out of my room now!" says Lindsay. She's still standing straight as a toothpick but with a more menacing look on her face. It's like the two of them have forgotten I'm in the room. An awkward tension fills the space. I long to say something to diffuse it but don't know what I'm supposed to say. I say nothing.

"Your mother called and she's not coming home tonight," says Greg. He gives a dramatic pause. "I figured you already knew that."

Lindsay sneers at him. "Yeah, I did. Don't feel like you need to babysit us, Greg. We're fine on our own. Right, Megan? In fact, Megan and I were just about to go out."

We were? I think that but don't speak it.

"I know the security code so it's cool if you want to spend the night elsewhere."

Greg laughs. "What, and miss all the fun? Sorry Linds, I promised your mother I would keep an eye on you and you know how she can get. She's so over-protective." He says the last part of that sentence to me, like he's sharing a secret.

"I bet my mom's more over-protective." I catch a weird look from Lindsay. Damn, I should have kept my mouth shut.

"Leave now, Greg. We're going to get ready."

"See you later girls. Don't do anything I wouldn't do," he laughs as he exits Lindsay's room.

Lindsay yanks out clothes from her mega-designer closet like there's no tomorrow.

"So, what's with you and your step-father?"

"Here, I think these will fit you. I need to get out. And in case you haven't figured it out, I hate him!"

"I pretty much got that."

"You're so lucky your parents are together."

I give a soft, hurt laugh. "Yeah, think again. My dad died when I was three and my mom…well, she's kind of busy." *Busy coping with MS that is.*

"Shit. I had no idea."

I shrug. "Most people don't. I'm a private person." More like I've got no friends and no one at school ever cared enough to ask.

"So it's just you and your mother?" asks Lindsay, urging me to try on a purple skin-tight shirt that I love but know will make my large breasts look like melons.

"Now, it's just Mom and me." *My brother...he's kind of out of the picture now.* She's holding the purple shirt out for me to take. I shake my head and pick up a dark brown shirt that looks a bit baggier.

"No way, Megan. This shirt was made for you. It will look fabulous on you. Trust me."

I look at Lindsay. Trust her. I don't even know her. Without a doubt she doesn't know me. With trepidation I take the shirt.

"You can change in the washroom if you like."

"Thanks, I will." I take the shirt and a black skirt she also hands me. There's a big smile on her face.

"I'm okay with wearing my own clothes, Lindsay. You don't have to give me yours."

"Are you kidding? Have you seen the amount of clothing in my closet? *Please.* You are doing them a favor. I didn't even know I had that purple shirt."

I laugh. "So are you saying your clothes have feelings?"

She laughs this time. "You're funny, Megan. At school you're different…so quiet."

"That's because no one talks to me, Lindsay." A pause fills the space. "Except you."

"That's not true," she says.

I shake my head. "It is. You just don't notice."

"Well, Megan, all that's about to change. You hang with me girl and with these clothes and that face…" She twists me around so I can look at myself in her mirror hanging off the back of her door, "others will discover you."

My face starts to feel hot. I don't want anyone to really discover me. I flash a smile at her and say thanks. Then I head into the washroom to yank the clothes on. There's a part of me that likes the feel of the designer fabrics on my skin, but as I stare at myself in the mirror I know something Lindsay doesn't. Change in my life has never been good.

The first time things changed Dad died. The second change was when Mom got diagnosed with MS. The third change happened a few months ago when my brother, Johnnie, got high and brought his best friend over for the night. That didn't go so well for me. Johnnie left the next day after I told him what happened and I haven't heard from him since. Thankfully he came back to visit Mom while I was at school. I have no idea what he said to her but she didn't ask me about him after that. The only thing I have now is his number which I've never called.

Things changed in our house after that. She only asked me once if we had a fight. I think he must have called and told her some excuse why he wasn't at home anymore. I never asked her. I used to be sick with worry about what he was doing but realized after two weeks of living through that hell, the only person hurting was me. Now, that worry has fizzled like stale ginger ale into simmering anger. For that alone, I hate my brother.

Chapter 5

Lindsay

I have no idea what came over Megan. One minute she was dressed like a queen, wearing my best clothes and I know she liked them, and then voilà, she said no thanks. Who the hell turns down designer clothes?

We make our way down Spadina Street. It's dark but as usual there are lots of people. Some homeless, a few Goths who followed us for a good block and enough weirdoes to fill a loony-bin. All of them, like us, are roaming the streets. In Halifax that wasn't always the case. On my street in Clayton Park most people stayed inside when it got dark. There was a gravel path there I could walk on and I often spotted deer on it. Not here. The only wildlife are squirrels the size of large housecats and rats, almost as big.

"I really don't want to go to a drugstore," I say.

"Me neither."

"How about a drink?"

"Coffee, right?" asks Megan. The way she says it gives me an idea.

"Have you ever tried to get into a bar?"

"Lindsay, anyone can go into a bar, we just can't order a drink," says Megan, like I'm nuts.

"Want to try?" I blurt out, feeling adventurous.

She's looking at me like I'm nuts and partly like she's up for trying it. "You serious?"

"I am now. Come on, there's this bar I heard of that's a bit dingy but supposedly Rebecca and Blair got loaded there last weekend."

"Are you kidding?" Megan's fidgeting with her sweater.

"Nope. We have to take a subway to get there. I still haven't figured them all out."

Megan pushes her bangs off her face. "Now subways I know all about. I heard you came from out East. Don't they have subways?"

I stop so abruptly a girl collides into me. She mumbles sorry and walks around us, her earphones still in place. "I came from Halifax. It's the biggest city in Nova Scotia and it's nothing like this place. They don't have subways. They've got buses but my mom would never let me take one. Here she seems to think subways are safer than buses. She of course would never set one foot on the platform." I chew my bottom lip, thinking I've said too much.

"I hate the subway. It always stinks like stale air and body odor. But buses here aren't as fast. I've never been outside of Toronto. You are so lucky you get to travel."

I wish I could tell Megan the truth. My mother's so busy I've never really travelled. I don't count our trip to Mexico as a vacation. The only thing I saw there were the four yellow-painted walls in my room. I heard from Mom the weather was great. She of course stayed at a nearby resort and popped in daily to brief me on her pool life. The only good part had been she'd ditched Greg. I originally thought she had done that because she believed me. Now I know different.

"You know what I miss the most about moving?" I fall into step with Megan who has slowed down.

"What?"

"Nothing."

I force myself to laugh. This is the role I'm supposed to play. Gone is the old Lindsay. Only the "new" Lindsay is allowed to take the subway, go to a bar and order a drink. The old Lindsay would be wallowing in self-pity and walking down that long dark road of why me? Not anymore. Wow, my psychiatrist would be so proud of me. Too bad she only hears the lies I'm allowed to say. Even telling her the truth has consequences.

"Here's the entrance to the subway. You sure about this Lindsay?" Megan's looking at me with a mixture of worry and hope on her makeup free face.

I stop. Take out my handy-dandy makeup bag and urge her to move to the side of the steps leading down to the subway platform. "Stand still and do not move. I'm only going to apply lipstick and black eyeliner. The makeup will make you look older."

I wait for her to complain. She doesn't. I apply my magic and flash the hand mirror at her. Megan smiles. I wish a bit of makeup could make me happy.

"You okay?" asks Megan, jarring me away from my dark thoughts. She's too perceptive.

"Fine. Lead the way." I follow her down to the platform. She's right. The place stinks of urine and body odor.

"Told you," she says, catching me off guard. How the hell did she know I was thinking of what she had said earlier?"

"You're wrinkling your nose so I know you're thinking I'm right. Let's just hope the subway comes fast. This place really stinks. I bet homeless people have been sleeping here."

"Really?" The thought repulses me.

"Of course. At least it's warm in here. However, most times the police kick them out. Ohh, feel that." She looks down at the grime-crusted floor. "That vibration means the subway will be here in a minute. You feel it, then hear it, then you see it."

A minute later she's correct.

"See, told ya."

She steps through the doors like a pro. Me, I still hesitate. It's not like I'm about to fall in between the space separating the platform and the subway but knowing it's there always makes my steps hesitant. Keeping my head up and ensuring my smile is plastered to my face, I walk into the subway thinking this is not exactly how I had planned our night.

The other thought echoing in my brain is that if my mother finds out she'll kill me. I resist the urge to laugh. I tried to die and she wouldn't let me. Instead, she made me promise to never talk about what happened. Then, to erase all evidence, we high-tailed it out of Halifax faster than one of her famous takeover bids to better pretend all is fine. Our lives are nothing but lies. I might as well add this night to my growing list of sins.

Chapter 6

Megan

Lindsay is sucking on the bottle of white wine like there is no tomorrow. "My turn." I swipe the bottle from her slippery fingers. She doesn't resist. I think all that hyper energy she had got diffused when we didn't even make it past the door of the bar. Guess we both look young for our ages. The bouncer laughed when we told him we were nineteen. His exact words were something like, come back in three years. Lindsay told him to fuck himself, while I urged her to move on.

Now my butt is frozen and I'm chilled to the bone. For early November we're lucky we're not sitting on snow. Another month and it will be Christmas. I wish I hadn't thought of that.

"You going to drink it or stare at it?"

"You, Lindsay are a surly drunk," I say. She barks a dry laugh and snatches the wine from me. Taking a large swig of it, she wipes her mouth when some of it drips down her chin.

Brandishing the bottle up in the air like it's a trophy she says, "At least I managed to get us this."

"I tried." And was mighty happy when I failed. I had thought she wouldn't get the guts to venture into the corner store. Wrong. She waited thirty minutes to gather her nerve but then sauntered in the place, looking like her usual million bucks self. The clerk didn't bat an eye. I know because I spied at her from the side window. Lindsay even flicked her hair over her shoulder like a pro. Then we hide our stash under my large jacket and took the subway back to her place. We never made it to her place though. Her bright idea—drink our illegal alcohol on the school grounds. Nothing like adding an element of danger to our strange night.

"My butt's frozen…you want to head inside soon, Lindsay? We could watch a movie now." I'm sure it's well after midnight but I'm desperate to get warm and inside. I hate scary movies and that's all she had picked earlier but at this point I'd take watching Scream or even Saw if it warmed me up.

"Almost done." Her voice sounds more slurred than it had a few minutes ago. I look at the wine she's guzzling in earnest and realize I've only had about a cup. She drank the rest of it.

When Lindsay stands she almost stumbles off the school steps. I'm glad I insisted we move to the back part of the school to drink our stash. I picked it because it's the darkest area.

"What the fuck are you two doing?"

Even in the dark I would know that voice anywhere. Instantly, I grab Lindsay before she topples down the steps. "Just hanging. What are you doing here, Peter?" I ask, hoping he'll leave us alone.

Normally I would want Peter Spencer to come closer just so I could get a whiff of his expensive cologne he wears at school. Even though our trendy school has a no scent policy not one student follows it, except me. My excuse for following it has been I keep with the rules. The reality is that's a lie. I'd love to wear expensive perfume but I love my mom too much to put her through that.

"Is that you, Lindsay?"

His voice is full of concern. God I hate that. As usual he doesn't notice me. Same old, same old.

"Yeah, it is, Peter. Go fawkooff," says Lindsay, brushing off my hand that's trying in vain to keep her standing. She stumbles down a step and Peter pulls a freaking Superman move. He's there to catch her so fast I want to hurl my disgust on his designer high-tops.

"Jesus, Lindsay. You're drunk. It's Monday night, what's going on? And why are you here, Megan?"

He's looking at me like I'm the culprit. I wish he had kept walking by us. Right now with him this close to us I can't help noticing how his brown hair looks messed. A vision of him lying warm in his bed hits me. My face flushes with warmth and even though it's dark where we are, I'm sure he notices.

"Let me go, Pete. Megan's sleeping over. Want to join us?" Lindsay leans more into Peter than I like.

"She's wasted. Why did you let her do this?" asks Peter.

"It just sort of happened," I say, meaning it.

"Well this is your fault as much as hers. If her parents find out they won't be impressed. You're lucky it's just me that walked by you two. What if a cop came by or something? Trust me, you don't want that."

The way he says it makes me wonder if he knows from experience how it would suck big time.

"I'm walking both of you home." His declaration causes Lindsay to laugh hysterically.

"What's so funny?" I ask Lindsay.

"He's our knight in shining armor, Megan. Good old goodie-two-shoes Peter Spencer will walk us to the door to ensure our safety…shit, this fucking sucks. Go away Peter. You're too good for the likes of me."

"What's she talking about?" Peter asks me.

I think we're having one of the weirdest conversations ever, but now that I'm up off that godforsaken cement step I've got the chills. "Let's just get to your house, Lindsay." I'm urging her to walk, trying hard to ignore the fact Peter's casting angry glances at me or the fact Lindsay's leaning her head on his shoulder. If getting drunk would have earned me one of Peter's shoulders I would have gladly had more of that stuff.

"Megan. I thought you didn't do this stuff. I thought you were good."

"Go fawk yourself Pete. You don't know us. Megan's great. She's *savvving* me tonight and for that she's my BFFFFF always," slurs Lindsay, her feet tripping along behind her. Peter's practically dragging her down the block now.

"It's BFF, Lindsay. You are so going to regret this tomorrow. You had both better show up for school tomorrow or I'm telling."

"What?" I almost stop, but if I stop Lindsay's likely to fall to the ground. I think for a second her eyes must be closed.

"Everything has consequences Megan. I'm helping you to the door but the rest is up to you. Get her in her room quick. But like I said, I expect to see you tomorrow at school. No excuses."

"When did you become such a prick?" I ask, glaring at him.

"Prick? Can't imagine you say that word a lot, Megan. It's not like you."

I shrug, knowing he can't see it, even though he's right.

Growing up around kids who swear like it's their second language, I long ago made a point of not using profanity. "Like Lindsay just said, you don't know us."

He stops at the bottom step to Lindsay's house. I can't believe we got here as fast as we did. I realize now if Peter hadn't shown up this trek would have taken me over an hour to drag Lindsay along.

"Just get her inside. I trust you Megan to do the right thing." The outside light is on and I notice he's staring at me with his bright blue eyes for a good minute. That look conveys more than his words ever could. He really does trust me. He shouldn't.

He let's go of Lindsay's almost limp arm and turns away from us. I watch him walk down the sidewalk. With the street lights on I notice his fashionably tailored black leather jacket, and how long his legs look in his designer jeans. He turns up the collar of his jacket. I wonder if he does that because he's cold or because it's fashionable. Peter is just like Lindsay. They would make the perfect couple. They are cut from the same cloth—rich. In that moment, I hate Lindsay, even though I know I shouldn't.

Chapter 7

Lindsay

I can't believe I let Megan talk me into going to school. What the hell was I thinking? My head is pounding and my stomach feels queasy. The double café latte I sucked back this morning is doing nothing to help.

"What the hell happened to you?"

Rebecca's voice sounds like a jackhammer in my head. "Keep it down. Why are you yelling?"

"Linds," she says, causing me to cringe. "I'm not yelling. You really don't look well."

"Yeah, and I don't feel well either," I mumble.

"If I didn't know you better I'd think you have a hangover," she laughs.

She's right on target but I'm not about to confess. I shut my locker and for once don't bother to check out my reflection in the mirror. Why bother? I looked like shit this morning and no amount of makeup helped. I even hauled out the expensive stuff Mom got for me from Japan. Adding that to my face only made me look more chalky-white. Megan helped me wash it off and honestly I would have flopped back down on my bed to snooze for another two hours but she was like a freaking hound-dog, making sure I got up to move my ass or else. The or else part is the only reason I'm here now.

"I just ate something that didn't sit well with me." More like drank an entire bottle of cheap white wine and now I wish I could purge.

"You should see the nurse and get a white slip so you can go home." Rebecca shuts her locker. Her eyes, as usual, dart to Blair sauntering down the hall with that jock-stride I hate.

"Have to go. See you in second period."

She doesn't wait for me to respond. Sometimes I wonder why

she's my friend. We are not one bit alike. Except for the money connection. Rebecca's parents are loaded. Old money, said my mother, with disgust. Unlike her they never had to worry about their business. My mom worked her ass off to get where she is, and while I admire that, I also hate her for it. Even with Mom's disgust with the notion of old money and people that inherit stuff like that without having to work for it, that didn't stop her from making an instant networking connection with them within a week of us moving here. My first impression of Rebecca hasn't changed. She was sweet and charming from the get-go but she's all fluff. Inside she likes to push the envelope way too much. If she really knew me, she'd think in her weird way, I was "cool" for trying to commit suicide. Trust me there was nothing cool about it.

Then I think Rebecca's a genius. For the first time that morning I feel a ray of sunshine with the prospect of getting a white slip that will send me home.

I'm almost at the nurse's office when I spot Peter as usual trying to convert more people to his committee. Ugh. There is no way I can hide or ignore the fact he's watching me like a hawk. At the door of the office he walks over to me.

"Going somewhere, Lindsay?"

Peter's play acting concern for my well-being is totally fake. What a jerk. I didn't believe Megan's story this morning until she described in detail what Peter wore. Knowing he's my curse for being here and feeling like shit, even though he wasn't the one drinking, makes me glare at him. My look is totally wasted on him.

He steps in front of me, effectively blocking my way. "Don't even think of asking for a white slip."

"Go away, Peter," I say, "And, move out my way."

He shakes his head. I get a whiff of his cologne and clutch my stomach. It's the same stuff Greg wears and it makes me seriously feel like hurling on his sneakers.

"Life isn't pretty Lindsay, but you should have thought of that last night."

"Jesus, Peter, what are you, Mr. Perfect, or something."

"Far from it. I just thought this lesson would be your easiest. I can't believe you and Megan were drinking last night."

"Shh!" I try stepping past him.

"What, you don't want everyone to know that you, Ms. Perfect, aren't so perfect?"

Okay, is he trying to piss me off just to annoy me? "Look, Peter. I never said I was perfect. Why don't you leave me alone and go fuck yourself."

He tisks at me, like a two-year-old. "Lindsay, you obviously weren't paying attention in health class, I can't fuck myself. However, if ever…"

I grit my teeth and know my eyes are wide open. I let him finish that sentence with silence. The idea of fucking anyone in general, let alone Peter, who stinks like my step-father, repulses me.

Peter laughs. "I was only kidding Lindsay. You don't have to look so disgusted. It ain't going to happen."

"That's one thing you got right. It ain't never going to happen. Now, get out of my way before I seriously give into my desire to hurl on you."

He backs up with my declaration. Sweeping his arm across his chest in an old-fashioned gesture, I think for a second he's on something. Then I dismiss that. Peter Spencer is just weird. He's also head of the anti-drug committee at our school and something of self-declared fanatic. Thank god I didn't sign up for that committee.

I open the door and step through the entrance into the nurse's office. I force a smile to my face. Even that hurts my head.

"Can I help you, Lindsay?" asks Nurse Munroe.

Like our blue and white school uniforms, Nurse Munroe rocks her old-fashioned white uniform, equipped with the pill-box hat. This is casual week, meaning no uniforms. Next week it's back to our boring knee-length pleated skirts and catholic-white blouses. Nurse Munroe, who is probably in her sixties, always wears a uniform.

Calmly, Nurse Munroe ushers me into her office and urges me to take a seat. I shut the door behind me, instantly feeling better. At my old school we didn't have a nurse. We had a guidance counselor I had to visit once. Mom made sure I never went back there. For that I was thankful. My old guidance counselor's room was nothing like this. The walls for one are painted a bright cheery yellow, there is a comfy leather sofa at one end and I'm sitting on a plush black chair. There's nothing remotely institutional about

Nurse Munroe's office. All of the nursing stuff is located in a side room, which she accesses. There's even a private washroom.

"I'm not feeling so well, Nurse Munroe."

I keep my voice lowered on purpose. Sitting back in the chair, I think about the lies I'm going to need to say to escape school. For a moment guilt swamps me. I told Megan I wouldn't bail on her. However, I never asked her to trust me. While I'm glad she spent last night at my house, it's not like we're going to be best friends or something. If Rebecca and the others knew Megan spent the night at my house that wouldn't go well. Best to pretend I don't know her.

"Well, I am sure we will figure out what's wrong. It's probably nothing. But, there are basic questions I ask all my students who visit here. So let's begin with the first, shall we?"

I nod, thinking *let's get this over with and give me that goddamn slip so I can claim my bed again.*

"When was your last period?"

I blink. She pushes out a laminated calendar. The months are outlined in black, clearly marked with the weeks in red and the days are color-coded in green. I stare at last month's outline thinking *Holy fuck. I am so screwed!*

Chapter 8

Megan

Rebecca's twirling her blonde hair, while leaning against Lindsay's locker. "Lindsay, say it isn't true."

"What?" asks Lindsay.

They don't notice me. That hurts. My locker door is open and since I'm at the far end of the hall they can't see me either. Thank god. I, however, can hear Rebecca and Lindsay perfectly clear.

"There's a rumor that you had Megan spend the night at your house last night. Are you nuts?" Even though Rebecca is attempting to whisper it's not working.

"Maybe," says Lindsay.

Is she saying maybe she's nuts, or it didn't happen? I try hard not to make a sound as I listen intently to what Lindsay says.

"Come on Rebecca, you know me. Would I seriously risk my reputation and have Megan spend the night at my house? Give me a break. By the way are we still all meeting up at the pizza joint tonight at six?"

The rest of their conversation doesn't interest me. I heard all I needed to hear. What the hell was I expecting? Oh, I know, just maybe I had a real friend in this freaking school. *Wrong, Megan. So Wrong.*

I wait until they leave before getting the courage to shut my locker door. The thought of sitting through class with Lindsay next to me makes me want to gag. I look down at the short, black skirt Lindsay insisted was made for me, knowing now she lied. That's all she ever does. I'm glad now I'm wearing my usual no makeup face.

Hiking my purse over my shoulder I make my way to class, wondering why I bother. I clutch my netbook close to my chest, knowing I will never fit in here. It wasn't like I wanted a social life when I applied, but now...now that I'm here it would be nice to have at least one friend. At my old school I had lots. Not anymore. That's the thing in my neighborhood. You dare to make a change, try something better with your life and instantly you get branded as a traitor.

Traitor to what? Living on welfare and going to food banks when you run out of food before the end of the month. Yeah, right. If that makes me a traitor then so be it. I realize today is Tuesday and at home we've got another week before Mom's welfare cheque will arrive in the mail. Tuesday also means after school I've got army cadets. Can't miss that, because that's the only reason I'm here and I can't miss class, either. As much as the idea of ditching class thrills me, that isn't how scholarships work. One black mark on my file and presto—I'm out of here. The only reason the school administration allows me to walk these extra-polished marble floors is because this Prep school had to fulfill its social conscience and allow people like me, who are from the "other side of the track" but who meet all their academic requirements, in. They don't make exceptions though when it comes to bad marks, missing class or anything else. That was made clear as the acne cream Lindsay gave me, when a week before school started I got a letter informing me of my acceptance. The list of requirements I had to fulfill and agree to with a signed contract was longer than the goddamn scholarship form I filled out in the first place.

I go to class. It might be the last place I want to be but it's the only way I can escape the fate of my poverty-stricken life.

Plunking my purse down beside me, I try hard to ignore Lindsay. Opening my netbook I turn it on. I might as well be invisible. She is looking straight ahead, and doesn't even let her eyes slide a glance my way. I can't help noticing how pale she looks. A part of me relishes knowing she feels sick. She was the one who got wasted last night. Not me.

When Peter walks in and sits on the other side of Lindsay I expect at any moment for our science teacher to order him to his usual seat. He doesn't though. Peter leans across his desk and looks at me. I really wish Lindsay wasn't between us.

"So what gives?" he asks.

I quirk my eyebrows at him. He can't be that dumb. Or maybe he can. Playfully he pokes Lindsay's arm.

"Get lost Pete."

"I see the nurse didn't send you home," he says.

"What?" I force Lindsay to look at me. I can't help notice her eyes look red, like she's been crying. The only person here who should be crying is me. I'm no baby though. Tough might as well be my middle name. Too bad it's Cornelius, which I seriously hate.

"I wasn't feeling well," says Lindsay. Her head is looking straight ahead and she's almost mouthing the words at me.

"Well, I'm not feeling well either. Think I'll visit the nurse next period."

"Oh no you don't. You two are in this together." The fact that Peter's smiling makes my stomach do flip-flops. He's gorgeous but when he smiles his two dimples are adorable.

"Leave Megan alone, Pete. Seriously. Find another hobby other than that anti-drug committee. You're becoming a major freak."

Lindsay doesn't turn her head to look at Peter. And just like me, I notice Peter hangs on to her every word. Why is Lindsay now sticking up for me? Not five minutes ago she ditched me and practically told Rebecca I wasn't at her house last night. What gives?

Not wanting to get into it in class I decide to keep my mouth shut. Ignoring Peter is hard, especially since I get whiffs of his cologne every once in a while. Lindsay ignores me for the rest of class.

As soon as the bell rings, I dart out of my seat. "I'll bring your clothes back tomorrow," I say to Lindsay, making sure my voice is quiet so only she can hear me.

She turns her head to look at me. I see her gulp, like she's trying to compose herself.

"Thanks. That would be great. Megan about last night—"

"Forget it. I know it never happened. I'm not stupid, Lindsay. I won't breathe a word of it to anyone."

I wait for her to deny it. To say I'm the stupid one for suggesting something like that. Instead, she packs up her laptop and slowly gets out of her seat. "Thanks for being so understanding. I appreciate it."

I nod. She walks away. That's it. Not one backward glance. What the princess wants, the princess gets. Even as I think that I realize Lindsay looks worse than she had this morning. She wasn't crying when I practically dragged her out of bed, but just now, when she nodded, she looked fragile.

Why that matters to me annoys the hell out of me. I don't have time for Lindsay's mind games. The drama in my life is enough. My eyes dart around to the girls walking in their designer outfits. So far I'm hating casual week. We're only doing it as a charity fundraiser for some international group I've never heard of. That uniform cost me over a hundred dollars and while it was expensive for me, it also made me relax. A uniform meant no one would discover I'm not into designer clothing. More like I can't afford them. Now, watching everyone walk around in their swanky clothes, I realize I stick out like a poor relation.

I notice Rebecca is once again chatting away with Lindsay. Blair's got his arm around Rebecca's waist and I swear to god his hand is half-way up the back of her shirt. She doesn't seem to mind. These girls, even if they knew my drama, wouldn't care. The only thing they are concerned with is fashion, sex and drugs. None of which are a part of my life.

Guess that makes me the outcast here. The only difference between the girls here compared to my old school, is in my old school Blair would have had his hand up the front of Rebecca's shirt and no one would have cared.

Chapter 9

Lindsay

Why did I come? I look around at the usual crowd in the pizza joint and wish I had stayed home. However, home meant facing lovey-dovey Mother who only has eyes for Greg. She barely even said hi to me. The only thing she did mumble to me, in-between hugging Greg, who had the freaking nerve to wink at me, *as if*, was to remind me not to be late. *Too bad I already am.*

"What took you so long?" Krista, who is more Rebecca's friend than mine, gives me a lame girl-hug. I can't help notice she and Rebecca are wearing matching, black skin-tight jeans and off-the-shoulder blue shirts belted with white studded leather belts that so belong in my mother's closet. That is wrong on so many levels.

"My mother came home…you know how it is." They have no idea whatsoever. I sit down on the hard plastic booth seat. There are four pizzas on the table. The only people eating as usual are the boys. Derek smiles at me, and blushes, which makes the zits on his nose stand out like Rudolph the Red Nosed Reindeer. Jeff doesn't make eye contact, because he's too busy playing some stupid game on his Blackberry. I haven't figured out why Jeff even hangs with Derek and Blair. He's not on the football team or any sport team for that matter and he barely talks to anyone when he's with us. But the three of them are like peas in a pod.

Blair casually waves at me while stuffing his mouth full of the meat lover's pizza which is loaded with onions. I grab a piece and it's almost in my mouth when Rebecca slaps my hand.

"Are you crazy? Don't eat that," she says, like I'm nuts. The only crazy people here are the girls who never eat. Tonight, screw that. For once, I'm eating the freaking pizza because I'm starved and two, it's not like I'm looking to get kissed. Far from it. If I never got kissed again I'd be happy.

I stuff the slice in my mouth, savoring the hot taste of a white onion.

"Ew, your breath's going to stink, Linds."

"Don't call me that," I mumble to Rebecca. As usual she ignores me and even though Blair's wolfed down half the onion-loaded pizza his breath obviously doesn't matter to her. Watching her chow down on his lips makes me ill.

"Keep squirming like that Becca…it feels good." Blair groans for show.

"You feel so good," says Rebecca, like we all don't know exactly what the two of them are doing gyrating on the plastic seat.

That's the other problem with being with Rebecca and Blair. They enjoy making the rest of the crew uncomfortable.

"Okay, what's the plan?" asks Derek, moving over in the booth to make way for Krista who had missed the kissing show. Since Derek and Krista are now an official item, I'm the odd one out. That's okay by me, but not by Rebecca or Krista.

As soon as the door opens I know I've been set up. I glare at both of my so-called friends. They remain oblivious.

"Tell me you did not do what I think you did." I grab another piece of pizza to devour.

Shrugging their shoulders, they try to look innocent. Krista might be able to pull that off but not Rebecca.

"Connor, what a surprise." Rebecca ushers him over to sit next to me. Since I haven't moved an inch to make room for him, he's left standing. That is until Rebecca kicks me under the table, forcing me to move.

"Nice to see you again, Lindsay," says Connor.

"You too, Connor," I say, not really meaning it.

He's another newbie at our school trying to fit in. I thought that might give us a connection. It doesn't. I will admit Connor is cute, if you like brown hair that has a curl to it that you know he fights with the use of gel. He's the tallest boy in our school at six-foot three. He tends to haunch a bit, like he's uncomfortable with his height. He's got broad shoulders most girls would love to get close to, but not me. Well, that's not entirely true. We tried last week to get close when we were all at Rebecca's house for movie night but things didn't go as planned.

"Want some pizza?" asks Krista, pushing a box toward him.

Connor shakes his head. "Nope, I'm good. Already ate."

"What did your mom make you eat tonight?" asks Rebecca.

I barely resist rolling my eyes. Instead I catch a passing waitress and order pop. Connor also orders one. And wouldn't you know it, it's the same brand as me. Plain old ginger-ale. They say ginger helps settle your stomach. Not sure it's going to work tonight but anything is worth a try once.

Connor smiles at Rebecca and when he does it makes him look exotic. The thing about Connor the girls love is his ethnicity. He's half South-east Indian, something he's proud of, and the other half is totally Irish-Canadian. He's got cinnamon-colored skin, making it look like he's got a perpetual tan, and almond-shaped light brown eyes. Think GQ material and that would be him.

His parents have their own tragic love story, which Connor is only too proud to tell anyone who will listen. His mother's family came from a poor rural village in India and at the age of five she was married in the traditional Hindu fashion to an older man. He died, making his mom an unworthy widow, even though they were never technically together. His father at the age of eighteen was on a hiking trip with his private school and one day when he was walking alone he discovered this exotic Indian woman crying. When he learned of her plight, that she was to become an outcast because of what happened to her, he made a bold move to help. I'm sure it helped that Connor's mother is a stunning beauty. Anyway, somehow or another Connor's father and this young woman made it to New Delhi and got secretly married. One tragic ending averted.

"Mom made her usual, dhal and spicy lamb," says Connor.

Both Krista and Rebecca groan with pleasure. Since I've never had Indian food I can't imagine the taste.

"Did you know that our own Linds here has never even tried Indian food."

I kick Rebecca under the table and mouth at her to shut up.

"So?" I say defensively.

"She came from Nova Scotia, that's her excuse."

Krista likes to pretend she knows everything about where I came from. The only thing Krista knows is what Rebecca tells her.

"For your information Krista, there are Indians in Nova Scotia."

Krista tisks at me. "Don't be silly. It's not like here."

When she says here, she's referring to Toronto's Little India, a place bustling with shops that sell exotic saris, spices, jewelry, and tempting food.

"Actually, I'm going to Nova Scotia in the summer for a two-week vacation," says Connor, looking at me like he'd like to say more. How about an apology for that night at Rebecca's house, big guy? Nope, didn't think so.

"That's nice," I say, not meaning it.

"Listen, Lindsay can I speak with you for a few minutes?" Connor gets up from the booth, making it clear to everyone he'd like a private tête-a-tête.

"Nope. I'm good." I stay seated, while ignoring Rebecca's heels. Honestly, if she kicks me one more time under the table I'm going to throw a piece of pizza at her.

"Please," he says, holding out his large hand like I'm about to take it.

"Don't be an ass, Linds. Go talk with him," says Rebecca.

I look at Rebecca and then Connor and understand instantly he told her what happened. That pisses me off.

"Fine," I snap, moving out of the booth and out the door of the pizza joint, forcing Connor to follow. At the side of the small shop, I lean against the cold brick building, noticing the litter lining the street, the stench of car exhaust and the amount of people milling about on the sidewalk. In Toronto's financial district it's hard to find trees, flowers or anything remotely unrelated to concrete or asphalt.

Before I can say anything, Connor says, "Listen, about last week. I'm really sorry."

"I…" I want to say more but can't. I know what happened outside at Rebecca's house was more my fault than his but it's not like I can confess how screwed up I am.

"Can we be friends again, Lindsay?" Connor makes it clear by his stance he's waiting for me to say yes.

"Listen Connor, it wasn't you. It's me."

He's shaking his head. "No, it was me. I pushed you. I shouldn't have…it's just that…"

He pauses, letting the filthy car exhaust fill our lungs. Thoughts of what happened last week swirl through me. We kissed. I thought if I kissed another guy it wouldn't make me feel dirty. It didn't work. I kept trying, hoping it would get better. Even when Connor's hand slipped under my shirt to touch me, I kept trying. The minute his finger brushed my breast I went rigid. He, however, didn't notice. Guess he was caught up in the moment, because he kept on slobbering at my neck, while his hands groped at me like there was no tomorrow. Only when he took a breath did he notice my steel-like stance and the fact I was crying. Even now, it angers me that I couldn't find my voice and I did the sissy thing and cried. *What is wrong with me?*

He shuffles his feet back and forth kicking wrappers out of his way. "It won't happen again. I promise. Friends?" He can't look at me when he says friends. His eyes are glued to the litter lining the sidewalk. He's clearly waiting for my acceptance.

"Sure. Friends. That's it though. Nothing more."

Connor flashes a smile. Any normal girl's heart would melt with that look.

"Thanks, Lindsay. It really bothered me that I made you cry."

"You didn't make me cry, Connor." The minute the words come out I know I should have kept my mouth shut.

"Okay, right." He doesn't believe me, but I'm thankful he doesn't pry.

The only people who make me cry are Greg and my mother. Both for different reasons

"Guess I'll have to be the one to break it to Rebecca that we're friends," says Connor, with a chuckle.

I know he's trying to lighten the mood and for once I appreciate the effort.

He kicks at a wrapper and then looks at me. "She's been trying to set me up since I moved here."

I roll my eyes. He laughs for real. The sound startles the pigeons attacking the empty wrappers.

I move my body from the cold brick to stand on both feet. My hand slides into my jean pocket to finger the note the nurse gave me. It wasn't a white slip to send me home. It's the name of an anonymous abortion clinic in the east end of town that has a no-ask policy and according to her, truly cares about their patients. Thankfully, Nurse Munroe didn't ask a lot of questions either. I think my shell-shocked look said it all.

"So, you really going to Nova Scotia?" I need to think about something other than the shit going on in my life.

"Yeah, my dad's brother just moved there from Calgary and we've always kept in touch with them. My cousin is about my age and we get together every summer."

"Where in Nova Scotia?"

"I think they said Halifax. Dad's brother took a job at one of their hospitals as Chief of Radiology. I'm going to see the Citadel and we're also going to visit Prince Edward Island."

For a moment I feel nostalgic for home. When I lived in Halifax, I only visited the Citadel once because of a school field trip. I thought it was boring as hell and we never made it to PEI because Mother-dearest was, like now, always working.

"Do you know where in Halifax?" I wonder what street they might live on.

"Some place in the south end. Not sure, why?"

"Nothing. Just wondered."

"Is that close to where you used to live?"

I can't help but laugh. Connor laughs along, not getting it. The lies of my so-called new life must be maintained. The south end isn't close to where I used to live. Even though I grew up in the middle class area of a fairly new subdivision, the public school I went to consisted of kids on welfare, gangs, druggies, hipsters and a bunch of other weirdoes, just like me.

"Yeah, sort of." Still fingering the note in my pocket, I say, "Let's go back inside. I'm frozen."

Connor makes a move to take off his dark blue Hollister hoodie. "Want my sweater?"

"Thanks. I'm good," I say, before he whips it over his head.

We go back inside and I can tell by the curious looks on both Krista's and Rebecca's faces they want to know the dirt.

"Everything good?" asks Rebecca, who at least has moved off Blair's lap.

I can't help notice Jeff has gone but I can't recall him leaving the store.

"I'll be right back." Connor sits in my spot so I can go to the washroom. Both Krista and Rebecca get up to follow me. I think of telling them not to bother but they won't listen.

Inside the girl's washroom they both start re-applying red lipstick to their already glossed up mouths.

Rebecca watches me as I move inside the privacy of a stall. "So, what's new?"

For a moment, I think about the package the nurse gave me. Hard to believe less than four hours ago I had to pee on a stick and wait for the results. I had prayed to God then for a miracle not to have this happen to me. I used to pray when Greg first started coming into my room when my mother was gone but I stopped believing in the power of prayer when Greg kept coming back. God let me down then and still has. The bright blue lines on the stick said I was positive—pregnant. You might as well have nailed me to the cross because there is no way I'm ready to deal with this.

"Everything okay in there Linds?" asks Rebecca, actually sounding like she's concerned.

"I'm going back out," states Krista.

From under the stalls I watch Krista's heels walk past my stall. Only when I hear the door close do I muster my courage and place my happy face back on.

"So, tell me. Did you and Connor make up?" Rebecca plucks at her bright pink bra strap that's showing through her off-the-shoulder shirt.

"Yeah. We're good."

"That's great. I'm glad that's all settled. We were all talking about how weird it felt with you not having someone."

I look at her, not believing she's telling me this.

"So now that you and Connor are an item, this will all work out."

"What are you talking about?" I fear she's going down a path I don't want to follow.

Rebecca opens the door to exit the washroom. She's not paying a lot of attention to me anymore. Blair and Derek are being dopes and they are now rough-housing it inside the freaking pizza joint. We're all going to get kicked out in about another minute. Rebecca just laughs at them. I think they're childish.

"I booked us a room at this motel in the east end and I told my mom I'd be spending the weekend at your place. It's all worked out. Derek and Krista, me and Blair and now you and Connor, it's perfect. My mom won't call your mother or anything like that, so don't worry. My mother actually trusts me. Disgusting, I know, but playing at being good does have its perks."

I am shaking. I can't believe she did this or thinks that's okay. I mean it doesn't surprise me because Rebecca is devious. But this. This is too far.

"Rebecca, I can't. It's not like you think."

"Listen, Linds, you don't want to let us all down now, do you?"

I can tell how she says it that if I do that, she'll ditch our friendship. To keep up with my perfect life I need Rebecca. Even my mother pointed that out when we met her and her family.

"Now, that's exactly how a daughter is supposed to behave." Mother made that remark after I suffered through a dinner party at Rebecca's house watching Rebecca flit around playing at being a hostess in training. No one but me knew she snuck outside for a joint.

"If you want to be my friend, do what I say and ignore what I'm doing."

Those were the exact words Rebecca said to me when I stumbled upon her getting high. I nodded, passing on the joint she offered. She took my nod for acceptance and that one movement cemented our relationship.

To not follow Rebecca makes you an outcast. I wonder for a moment what my mother would hate more—me being pregnant or a social outcast. Then again, at my new school, if anyone knew I was pregnant I would be "the" outcast. At my old school, they'd tell me to add my name to the growing daycare list.

"So we're all good?" asks Rebecca.

As usual I nod.

Chapter 10

Megan

I take my time getting home from school. I have lots to think about and I seriously don't want to be interrogated by Mom. Not that she's being mean when she asks me a ton of questions about my day, it's just that sometimes I want to keep things to myself. Well, that's not entirely true. If she knew half the stuff going on with me, she'd probably lock me in my room.

I unlock the door to our apartment and dump my backpack next to my shoes by the mat. I make a mental note to take it outside by the back door of the apartment building to give it a good shake. Our apartment building is only four stories and we're on the first floor for obvious reasons. Brown-brick is layered with stained siding making it look dated and in need of repairs. The fact that half of the paint around the wooden windows is peeling screams major makeover.

"Mom, I'm home."

No answer.

I dart into the living room, feeling my heart thud in dread. No Mom. Skidding down the well-marked hallway I stop at the bathroom door. The door's shut something impossible to do with my mom in her wheelchair. No privacy in our house for obvious reasons.

I attempt to open it. No go. "Mom, you in there?"

Of course she's in there. I bang on the door hoping to get her attention. Sweat trickles down my back and I feel nauseous. "Mom, I'm coming in."

Using my strength I push at the door, slowly moving the old wheelchair out of the way. When there's enough room for me to slide my body through I do. Mom's fallen off her chair. She's done this a few times in the last little bit, but never did it make her go unconscious. My eyes dart frantically around the small room. I absorb stupid details. Her toothbrush is lying beside her with its bristles down on the floor, the caps off the paste, her forehead is bleeding. I kneel down even though I'm shaking with fear. I'm praying with all my might for her to be okay. I know she's not, but this…this I can't deal with. The blood is fresh so I'm hoping she hasn't been out too long.

Not knowing what to do, I call the one number I think of. The phone rings a dozen times before I hang up. Then I call 911. The dispatcher talks me down and walks me through the scene: where we live, what's our apartment number, is my mom breathing? Shit, I don't know. I go back into the bathroom and notice her chest is moving. Relief makes me breathe easier. The dispatcher tells me the paramedics will be there in five minutes. I'm to wait on the line with her. She wants me to listen for the ambulance, like only a freaking moron could miss the wail of the sirens as they pull up to my place. Immediately it's like I'm a star and everyone is staring at me as I usher them like a madwoman into the building. My face heats with shame as I let the paramedics into our place. They barely talk to me. Instead they make their way to the bathroom, maneuvering their bulky bodies around the old stained banana boxes that are filled with my brother's things. I follow until they ask me to leave the space to give them room to work.

One of the paramedics moves the wheelchair up and into the bathtub. Why didn't I think of that?

I nod at them as I make my way back down the hall. I don't realize I have a death grip on the phone until I force my numb fingers to put it down on one of the boxes. A few minutes later they emerge, wheeling my mom out on a gurney. She's strapped down with a wool blanket covering her all the way up to her chin. There is an oxygen mask covering her mouth and what looks like a portable IV is hooked up to her.

"Is she going to be okay?"

"Not sure. Any idea how long she's been out?"

I shake my head. This is all my fault. If I didn't take my time coming home, she might be okay.

"She's going to probably need a CAT scan and she'll be in the hospital for a few days. You want to come along."

I nod again, fighting the tears threatening to mark me as a cry baby. No way. I make my way toward the ambulance.

"Your Mom going to be okay, Megan?"

Mrs. Burrows lives next door to us. Normally when I go out I let her know. She's got a key and likes to keep Mom company. My mom doesn't really like her, but she was brought up to be nice to everyone so I always use Mrs. Burrows when I know I'm going to be staying late at school or studying at the library. Another layer of guilt eats at me.

I notice Mrs. Burrows is in her gym clothes, blue velour that was outdated a decade ago. Like everyone in the building, she too lives on a fixed income. When it's fixed you tend to worry more about paying the rent, buying food and paying your electrical and water bills. Clothing becomes fourth rated.

"Not really sure, Mrs. Burrows. I'll keep you posted."

"You should give Johnnie a call."

I nod. I called him but he didn't answer. As I make my way to the front of the ambulance to accept my ride to the hospital, I'm wondering why Johnnie didn't answer. I'm not sure how I feel about seeing him. Dealing with Mom is hard enough. Dealing with the shit that comes with Johnnie, well that's way more complicated.

I'm not allowed in the room with my mom when we get to the hospital. I feel like a lost button, loose and useless. One of the nurses tells me it might take a while. She asks me if there's anyone I can stay with. I say yes, a little too fast. Luckily, she's busy and my lie saves me from trying to figure out what I'm supposed to say. There is no one else. It used to be me, Mom and Johnnie. Then Johnnie found cigarettes, alcohol and drugs. He so far into gang life even I hear about his escapades and while it might make my skin crawl, knowing what he's now doing, I try to pretend otherwise.

Not knowing what to do I make my way to the cafeteria. My no buying coffee mantra I was on yesterday gets thrown out the window. Now that I've come down from the high I was on being scared to death Mom was dead, I'm feeling shaky and my head feels like it's a zit in need of popping.

"What are you doing here?"

The voice causes me to spill half the coffee off the side of the Styrofoam cup. Shit.

"Peter, what are you doing here?"

He flicks his eyes at me, probably noticing my state of stress. "I asked you first."

"Waiting." I hope he'll leave it be.

He does. I watch him help himself to a cup of java and we both make our way to the line to pay. At the cash the lady says I owe her two dollars. It's then I realize in my haste to climb inside the ambulance I forgot my backpack, my purse and my keys. I feel my face flush with embarrassment.

"I've got it." Before I can protest, Peter's pays the cash lady

I can only nod. Mumbling a thank you, I make my way to a hard plastic booth, hoping he'll continue on to wherever he was going. No such luck.

I slide myself into the seat and take a gulp of the brew. Surprisingly it's not that bad.

"I know it's pretty good. And for that you can thank me, Peter Spencer." He gives a mocking laugh, but it's a joke I don't get.

"What are you doing here?" I'm trying to figure out why Peter's at the hospital.

"My dad gets me Tuesday and Wednesday so I have to wait here for a good hour until he's finished. That is if I'm lucky."

"Your dad?"

He looks at me like I'm stupid. At this point I feel it.

"Dad's head of Emergency here. When it's busy, like today, I'm in for a longer wait."

Peter waves to one of the cafeteria ladies. She's easily forty, but he winks at her and she winks back. What the hell?

"That my dear is the reason you are drinking good coffee. That's Mary. She's in charge of the kitchen. Trust me, after years waiting in a hospital, you get to know lots of people."

"So you're saying you getting to know Mary is the reason the coffee is good."

Peter takes a sip to prove his point. "Yup."

"Just how well do you know Mary?" I ask, fighting back my smile.

"That's between Mary and me. Now, want to answer my first question?"

I pretend I have no idea what he's referring to. I finish my coffee in record time and start to move from the booth.

"Thanks again for getting Lindsay to school. I can just imagine how hard that was this morning."

If he's waiting for me to spill the jelly beans he's about to be disappointed. "I've got to go." I want to stay but know I can't. With how my day has been going I'm liable to talk and talking about me and who I really am is not something that will ever interest Peter Spencer.

"Stay. I've got another hour to kill," he says.

I laugh, startling him. "If that's supposed to get me to stay you are seriously mistaken. By Peter."

"Call me Pete."

My heart trips over. I heard Lindsay call him Pete and I had longed to the other night. I might fantasize about Peter but in his world, a girl like me doesn't exist.

"Yeah, gotta go Peter." I give him a small wave while I dart out of the cafeteria like there's a flea on my sweater.

I make my way up to Emerg, wondering if Peter will follow. Part of me almost wishes he had. The minute I get close to the waiting room I'm glad he didn't.

"What the hell, Megan. Why didn't you call?"

Johnnie's voice rings accusingly through me. That's all he has to say to me after what happened.

All the rage I've held inside since he left without a word springs free. "Fuck you Johnnie. I called. You didn't answer."

Chapter 11

Lindsay

After school on Wednesday turns out to be worse than my head-pounding, nauseous all-day, Tuesday. Honestly, I should have stayed home. That however, isn't going to happen. Mother waited up for me Tuesday night just to "talk". Her famous word for me listening to her while she speaks. Nothing new there. I gave up trying to talk when she gave up listening and that was a long time ago.

Now, I've curled up in an antique chair my shrink said came from her grandmother. I can picture that. It's old, like well over a hundred years. It has painted gold lion feet that hold it up and the deep chocolate brown is embossed with small dark red roses one can barely see in the design, but it's soft and comfy. It's also close to the fire.

My shrink doesn't look like a shrink and this place feels more like how a home is supposed to feel than an office. Again looks are deceiving. Ms. Pepper-Slaunwhite could pass for someone's grandmother. Her gray hair is artfully coiffed up on her head. Today, she's wearing a black fashionable sweater dress with a white wrap around her shoulders and she's got glasses that either perch on her small nose or hang loose around her neck. Her flawless skin is something any aging model would kill for, and her bright blue eyes have adorable crinkle lines around them. I bet she's at least fifty. She always smells the same. Or maybe it's her office. *Whatever*. The minute I walk through the front door of her house, yes, we meet actually at her house, I'm always hit with the smell of baking. It never fails to unnerve my mask with a longing for a real home and real mother. And the worse part about Ms. P, that's what I get to call her, is she seems to genuinely care about me. I hate that worse than the lies I spew. I always leave her place feeling hollow. It's almost like she knows I'm faking it.

Ms. P pushes the plate of peanut butter cookies toward me. "And how are we feeling today?"

Peanut butter is my favorite and the no nuts policy at school has been upping my cravings for the forbidden. I devour two of the cookies before I flash my practiced smile.

"Good," I mumble. I learned early on in these fake sessions it's never good to say too much. Usually I let her led—ask the questions until the grandfather clock chimes my hour is up. The only certificate on her wall detailing her credentials is one dated from 1968 from the University of Langley, California.

Mother made a point of letting me know that Ms. P is famous in her own inner circle and only takes on discreet clients, who wish to keep their problems to themselves. I had naïvely thought that was my cue to tell the truth. The minute we pulled up in front of Ms. P's stately home, my loving mother made it clear as my best concealer she expected me to get things off my chest with Ms. P, but not to tell tales. I don't know what I expected but that hadn't been it.

I didn't say anything. Nodding is always the easy way out when dealing with Mother. And just like Rebecca she gets her own way.

Ms. P takes a cookie, nibbling on it. "So, anything new you'd like to talk about today?"

New. How about freaking massive NEW! How about I'm preggers and can't tell anyone. How about I hate my step-father and think about killing myself every frigging day. "No. Not much new." I slide back into the comfy chair.

"Wow, nothing new at school. Man when I went to school all kinds of shit was happening. People skipped classes, smoked up, did drugs, slept around, well it certainly wasn't boring in my day." See, that's the thing about Ms. P. she looks like a grandmother but she talks my language.

"Well, I never said it was boring."

"No you didn't did you? Why don't you tell me in your own words what's going on with Lindsay?" She doesn't sit back in her chair. Instead she braces her hands on her legs eagerly waiting for me to tell her something of meaning.

For a moment temptation looms in front of me. I grab another

cookie before I lose my control and stuff it in my mouth.

I watch her settle back in her chair. It's like she knew I debated telling the truth once but thirty seconds passed and that moment vanished. Forty minutes later I'm tugging on my coat when a piece of paper falls out of my pocket. Ms. P picks it up. My heart's hammering away and I'm sure my eyes show my panic. The note is folded in half but the words are totally visible. The top half says a clinic's name I'm hoping she's never heard of.

She hands me the paper without a word. She doesn't need to. Her eyes say it all. She knows my secret. Too bad it's not the dirty little secret I wish she knew. My hands are shaking as I clutch my purse. I fumble as I finish buttoning my jacket.

"I think we should see each other next week Lindsay." It's not a question. I'm caught between reminding her we only meet once a month, but know that's not going to wash. She's waiting for my reaction. It's not like I'm stupid. I know who pays her bills. My mother.

At the door, I say, "I'm kind of busy next week."

"I know you'll find time. Say, same time and day. You do know that everything that gets said here is strictly between you and me. No one—not even your mom will ever know what you say to me in confidence."

Yeah, I was soooo born yesterday. Not! "It's not like you think." The minute I blurt out the words I feel the beginning of my long list of lies start to unravel, like how my favorite sweater got ruined—one lose thread and it never was the same again.

"I don't think anything." She doesn't ask me anything else. Those are her parting words to me. My hand turns the old-fashion brass door knob.

"See you next week Lindsay," says Ms. P.

I don't nod. Not here. I might tell lies but nodding, would make her just like Mom and she doesn't deserve that.

I wish for freedom but escaping Ms. P's sharp, penetrating questions isn't the type of freedom I need. A clean slate would be nice, but Mother's not open to dealing with what happened and why. She certainly can't deal with the circumstances of my current situation and neither can I.

That's why I booked an appointment for next week at the clinic. Nurse Munroe said I should talk to someone about it.

Actually she pointedly told me to talk to the to-be-dad, citing he had a say in my choice. I laughed in her face because there is no way in hell that's happening. Lucky for me she answered my one question.

"Where can I go for an abortion without my mother finding out?" She had pursed her lips slightly in dismay—not shocked as I thought she might be—but Nurse Munroe didn't hesitate to write out the name of the clinic, directions and a telephone number. For that I'm grateful.

There's not much in my life that I have control over. Mother took dying from me. Greg took my childhood innocence but this…this is my decision. The only person making it is me. Why that makes me feel so alone sucks big time.

Chapter 12

Megan

Normally Wednesday night is something I look forward to. Not tonight. I'm too exhausted and because I didn't iron my uniform perfectly, I now have the joy of polishing all the brass in the place. *God, this sucks.*

I basically spent most of Tuesday night at the hospital with Mom. She's going to be okay, but the hospital is keeping her in for observation for a few days. That's a good thing, but what's not good is the fact Johnnie has returned home. At the moment he's staying in Mom's bedroom and so far we've avoided each other. I couldn't help but notice how the young nurses checked him out. Gone is his shy demeanor. He actually flirted with the nurse while Mom lay in the bed hooked up to an IV. I'm glad she was out cold. Flirting isn't Johnnie. The new tats on his arms aren't Johnnie either but I can't say that to him. I wonder in more ways than one what drove Johnnie to join the gang. Was it money? He's sporting new threads and his wallet is jammed with twenties. He actually tossed one my way when I complained I was hungry and that I had left my purse at the apartment. When he and the nurse cozied together for a smoke break I wanted to scream at him. However, my earlier remark didn't register to him so why bother trying.

I march over to my commanding officer and salute. "Finished, Sir." I make sure my voice is clear.

Master Corporal Windemere tells me to stand at ease. "Everything at home okay, Megan?"

See that's the bad thing about having the cadets as your second home. People get to know you and that familiarity can be both a blessing and a godsend. Tonight it's hell.

I'm glad we're in the privacy of his office. It's small and stark but the framed family pictures on his desk tell you everything you need to know about Master Windemere. I tell him about my mom being in the hospital. He already knows she has MS. He's the father figure I never had. In fact, he's got a daughter who was born on my b-day, so I think he likes to play dad to me. It was Master Windemere who recognized my skills, urging me to move up the reserve ranks, and further pushed me to apply for a scholarship to attend another school. One of the perks with the cadets is that they pay you to go to summer camp. I spent four weeks in training last summer and earned over three hundred dollars. That certainly isn't much to the Lindsays and Rebeccas of my world, but to me, that money meant I could buy a pair of jeans, new underwear and socks, two new shirts and a jacket from Wal-Mart.

"You take care of yourself and your mom, okay Megan? If you need anything give me a call. So how's the new school coming along?"

I wish I could jump up with joy and say it's great. Mustering a tired smile, I say, "It's okay." I don't mean it but luckily he buys my line.

"I'm sure it's hard for you. Giving up your friends from your old school is never easy. Have you made any new friends?"

Gulping, I'm quick to nod. "Yup." I think for a moment of Lindsay and wonder what she's up to tonight. She's probably hanging with Rebecca and the "in crowd."

"And your marks?"

"Straight A's," I say. A real smile lights up my face. And that's what I've got to think about always. Getting excellent marks will take me places.

When he hands me a brochure for summer training my mind's still thinking of Lindsay. He points out a new option for summer camp he thinks will be good for me. It's in Halifax, Nova Scotia. I almost laugh out loud. What are the odds of that? Me, going to visit Halifax, the place Lindsay comes from…it almost feels like fate is toying with me.

I take the brochure, say a few more polite words to Master Windemere and pack up. I've got twenty minutes to walk three blocks to my subway stop. It's dark, even though the street lights attempt to brighten the sidewalks. There is litter everywhere; blowing paper, empty pop cans and beer bottles line the sidewalk which is starting to get overgrown with brush. This isn't the best neighborhood. Since the area I live in isn't great, the fact that walking through the hood scares me shitless doesn't deter me. I need the cadets. It's the only thing we can afford. It didn't cost a thing to join and the uniform was free, plus the hot lunches on Sunday work for me. And, I like it. Just like making straight As, the army fits my personality. The fact I can't let anyone know at my Prep school has nothing to do with the cadets and more to do with the fact kids at my new school don't have to work or worry about the cost of uniforms. They all get hundred dollar allowances from their parents and think nothing of raking up credit on their parents' plastic either. My mom has never had a credit card and we have to stretch a hundred and fifty dollars for two weeks to cover food and heat.

When the crunch of boots echoes in my head, fear coats my skin causing a clammy sweat to form under my sweater. My feet automatically walk faster and so do my boot followers. Shit.

When I notice a group of teens merge up ahead out of a side alley, my eyes dart frantically behind me. *Great, it's a tag team.* I count six in total. They're all wearing dark jeans and black jackets along with dark wool caps that cover their foreheads. You'd think those were worn to keep their heads warm but the reality is they wear them so they can pull the cap down to cover their faces.

"Why lookie here, a little girl walking all alone. Didn't your mom tell you this area ain't safe?" says the one marching toward me with a swagger that would make an old cowboy proud.

"I don't want any trouble." I think fast about darting to the other side. I'm pretty sure the guys getting closer to my back would tackle me.

"We don't want trouble either chickie, now do we?"

The swaggering wannabee-cowboy is so close I can see his face. He's probably only a few years older than me but living by the rules of the street has given him a hard-core look no amount of therapy could erase. His eyes are brown and he's white with enough pock marks on his face to make my skin crawl. About six-foot two he's tall, skinny and trying to act big and mean. I'm worried he'll pull off mean with ease.

When a car screeches to a halt, we all look. When I see who saunters out looking like he's about to kill someone I'm both relieved and then worried.

"What the fuck is going on here?" asks my brother, Johnnie,

getting close to me but also close to the guy blocking my path.

"Fuck off Johnnie. We're not on your turf," says the guy, who I know Johnnie's going to beat the shit out of. I've seen Johnnie lose it and it ain't pretty. I don't want that to happen.

"Johnnie, it's okay. They were letting me pass."

"Shut up Megs. Get in that car and keep your mouth shut."

He pushes me toward the smart looking red Porsche that has me wondering how much it must have cost. I think about the fact that last month mom and me lived off a box of saltines for two days until she got her welfare cheque so we could buy more food. I try hard to think the car means nothing, probably isn't his, but the minute I settle inside the passenger seat I know that's not true. Every piece of tacky car accessory inside screams Johnnie, right down to the plastic Elvis he's got stuck on the inside dash and the goofy dream weaver dangling from his mirror.

"Lock the fucking door, Megs," he calls after me. I do. I don't realize my fingers are shaking until I have to force them to follow his orders. I keep my eyes peeled to the flickering streetlight in front of me. I watch four people run away and know Johnnie's not about to let the guy who talked to me escape. I try not to picture what he's doing to them and fail.

It feels like I'm sitting there for hours, but the reality according to the radio he left on is that fifteen minutes later he's done. Johnnie opens the driver seat and sits down. He doesn't say a word. His knuckles are bleeding and he's got a nasty slash on his right cheek, but he doesn't once wipe away the blood. He slams the car into drive. We peel out of there faster than how Lindsay yanked the mud wrap off my face. She said it would hurt less if we did it her way. Her way hurt like hell.

"Slow down, Johnnie."

He ignores me. We zoom through the streets and I'm counting seconds until a blue and white will haul us over.

"Johnnie, slow down, now! You want the cops on us?"

My shout finally registers. He slows to a normal speed but doesn't say anything. I can't find it in me to ask what happened. A large part of me doesn't want to know.

Only when he parks in the back of our building does he speak.

"That's a bad neighborhood, Megs. You're not walking there again."

My laugh is dry. "Are you trying to play big brother now?"

"I'm not kidding." He ignores my jab.

"In case you haven't figured things out Johnnie, I have a life. And you are not in it."

I get out of the car and slam the door. He's out of the car and in my face so fast I back up.

"I fucked up. You happy? I was stoned and out of my mind. I didn't clue in. I didn't know…fuck, this is all so fucked up." He steps away from me, his hands running through his rusty-brown hair and then he shoves them inside his pockets. I notice he's wearing expensive distressed jeans. I look down at my black worn gym pants that have a hole in each knee and feel pissed. He needs a good hair-cut. The blood has finally stopped dripping from his facial wound.

"Is that your 'sorry', because that sucks on all levels." I'm pleased when he takes two steps back from me. Johnnie angry is not something I want in my face.

"What do you want me to say, Megs? Tell me. I'll say it."

I chew on my bottom lip, trying hard not to cry. I told myself that night when he came home with his friend, both stoned out of their minds, that everything would be fine. It didn't work out that way.

His friend, in the middle of the night, raped me. To this day I swear I can feel his large hand clamped tight over my mouth. He stank like hashish and body odor and no amount of showering has erased that stench off me. He told me Johnnie wouldn't believe me—that it would be my word against his. Out cold from the drugs, I watched Johnnie sleep while his friend took my innocence. Worst part of it was his friend had always creeped me out. I had told Johnnie that a number of times and begged him not to let him sleep over. Johnnie told me to shut up and mind my own business.

In the morning I waited for his friend to leave and then quietly told Johnnie what happened. The tears came that time, but when Johnnie called me a bitch, saying I was nothing but a fucking liar, the faucet of tears stopped. Anger rooted itself deep inside of me. That was the only time in my life I screeched at Johnnie. I told him to leave. To get out of our lives and not to come back. Mom got upset but we both knew to keep our mouths shut about what we were fighting over. He left that morning. Now he's trying to play the oh-so-caring big brother and I'm not the same sister he left that morning months ago without a backward glance. I've grown up. The world is not fair and as long as you know that life goes on.

"Nothing. There's nothing that you can say that will ever make me feel better, Johnnie. Nothing. You get that." For the first time in a long time I tell the truth, hoping the weight of my words register. "What happened fucked us all up. You. Me and Mom. And it's because of you Johnnie. Because you wanted something more, the quick and fast way. That's how life is for you. You never think of the consequences. You brought your friend over when I told you not to. You chose him over us…over family."

He's hanging his head and it's then I notice he's trying not to cry. "You're right, Megs. You're right. I fucked up good. I'm not like you. Never was. I'm not smart in school like you and for people like me, life is the hard road. You want to know what those boys were going to do to you?" His eyes, green like mine, look at me. His are bloodshot from holding the tears at bay. Mine now weep openly.

I shake my head at him. I don't want to hear it. I figured out what was going to happen when I heard the boots walking behind me. While there was a part of me totally terrified with the knowing of what was to come, that dead part living inside of me also screamed that maybe I deserved it.

"They were going to gang rape you just for fucking fun. That's what they do."

"Is that what you do?" I challenge him, wanting him to see how I see him know.

"No. Never that. After what happened…" there's a long pause. I watch him curse under his breath, while he shuffles his feet around. Again I notice he's wearing expensive high-tops.

"Shit, fuck. I'm all messed up. But never that. And there isn't a minute that goes by Megs when I don't regret—"

"What happened," I supply the words for him, thinking those same thoughts.

He nods, wanting my understanding which I can't give.

It doesn't make me feel relief. Nothing ever can do that anymore. "I knew what they were going to do, but you Johnnie, you brought your friend in to our house and he raped me, not them! Worse, when I told you, you didn't believe me. Your gang friend is more your family than your own blood. That day when you left us, something inside of me died. And, that Johnnie is all your fault."

I walk past him, knowing I've lost him for good.

Chapter 13

Lindsay

I try hard not to notice Megan when she dumps her stuff in her locker. She's angry at me, but I've got enough drama in my life and dealing with her hurt feelings is something I can't handle. I wish I didn't feel like shit because of it.

"This, my dear is for you."

Peter attempts to paste a sticky note on my locker. Instantly, I peel it off. I don't bother to read it.

"That hurt my feelings," he says, like I care. The stench of his cologne causes my stomach to churn and I start to feel that cold sweat that tells me I'm about to dislodge my power bar breakfast.

"Leave me alone, Pete." I shut my locker door and attempt to walk past him.

"Since I thought you might try something like that, here's another one." He has the nerve to tape the sticky note to my laptop cover. "And in case you're thinking of not showing up, I wouldn't."

I don't move for a full minute. "Are you blackmailing me?"

He chuckles. "Yup, I am."

I get through the day at school, barely. After school I call Mother and cancel our pretend fun shopping spree. I never find it fun and shopping became mandatory after the "incident". If my mother could buy a perfect daughter I'm sure she would have disowned me years ago to get top of the line.

I hate Peter. That's what I think as I follow his damn Google map instructions. I thought we'd be meeting at the school for his anti-drug committee but oh joy, no. I'm actually being blackmailed to attend a real anti-drug meeting. After walking ten blocks I finally find the damn place. It's inside Smithers Southside Recreational Center, a place I've never ventured inside before and honestly, didn't even know existed.

At the steel door which has been painted a colorful orange I stop. Why am I doing this? What's the worst that could happen if my mother finds out I was drinking? So what if she freaks out on me. The thing with my mother is she layers on the guilt like a good painter. One layer and I'm okay but after listening to her monologue an hour later I always feel like shit.

Yanking my black beret lower, I open the doors and walk inside. The boom of loud music fills the space. I walk up the short flight of stairs and follow the music. Another orange door to open. Inside, the scene is not what I expect. Peter is the one in control of the music. He's basically set up a DJ system and between the overlay of rap I swear to god I can hear a song from the Wizard of Oz. There are twelve kids moving about on stage doing I have no idea what, and they look as lost as I feel.

One of the kids spots me and that's when Peter does. At the same time the door opens behind me and in walks Megan.

"What are you doing here?" I ask.

She doesn't say anything. Instead she holds up the same sticky note Peter gave me. Guess he likes to blackmail in pairs.

"I'm so glad you both came." Peter's smile is slightly different than his at-school "I'm the best" one he normally wears. For a second he looks vulnerable.

Megan walks past me, muttering, "You didn't give us a choice." I can't help noticing she's wearing the same clothes she had on when she came to my house. Weird. Her brown hair looks like it could use a good wash and she looks tired.

"This," says Peter, opening his arms wide, "Is going to be our project."

Okay, now I have no idea what he's talking about. The kids, who look like they are between the ages of ten and twelve, stare at us like we're the freak show. I'm starting to feel they're right.

"Okay, so out of here." I attempt to leave, which once again forces me to almost collide with Peter.

"Not so fast. I need you both. I have decided to enlist the two of you to help me in this project."

Megan grabs a worn wooden chair and sits down. "Peter, what are you talking about?"

I like that she gets down to business. That suits me fine. Peter launches in to what I swear to god must be a practiced monologue about the rec center, the kids and wanting to put on a new age Christmas play that has me cringing. Sadly, the more I listen the more I begin to understand what he's asking of me and Megan. So much for thinking this had anything to do with his anti-drug committee.

"No way, Pete. This is your baby and you're on your own," I say.

"What exactly do you expect us to do?"

Once again Megan takes the lead to fish out more information. I should leave while I can but some invisible glue has me stuck stupid on the spot.

"I really need help with the dance routine. See, I'm only good with the music." I have never heard Pete sound sheepish and for once it makes him seem genuinely real and caring. He runs a hand through his brown always rumpled hair and I try to see what the girls at school see in him. I mean, I know he's good looking but honestly the way he acts at school with his freaking no drug lectures, makes him downright annoying. The side of Peter I'm seeing now unsettles me. When one of the kids jumps down off the stage saying she needs help with her dance moves, Peter flashes a smile at me and Megan.

"These two gals are going to help you, Ashanti. We will so rock this play." He bends down so he's almost at eye level with the petite girl who looks at him in wonder. She's kind of cute if you like that puppy dog look she's mastered.

Peter stands up, motioning to me and Megan to follow him to the side of the large room. "This play is something the kids came up with as a way to help raise money for the rec center. This place needs to raise thirty thousand dollars by January or else the community center will be forced to close. It's the only place these kids have for a free after school program. I'm not asking a lot from you two."

Megan scoffs at him like he's barking mad.

"Okay maybe I am, but I know you two can help. You are both talented and you owe me." Now that sounds like the Peter I know.

"Peter, I don't know anything about dance moves," says Megan.

"No, you don't but Lindsay, you said you were a dancer before you moved here, right?"

Damn, I had said that to the class when we were forced to introduce ourselves on day one. Dancing at one time meant a lot to me. But even that changed once Greg entered Mom's life. *Note to self, keep your mouth shut the next time you start a new school.*

I give a slow nod, not wanting him to think I'm buying into helping, because I'm so not.

"And Megan, I know you are a talented artist," says Peter.

Megan blushes ten shades of lip gloss red.

"Not really," she says, fidgeting on her seat like she's nervous.

"Come on. I see you doodling all the time in class. And in art you made that amazing Monet impression which totally rocked. These kids need someone to help them paint a few backdrops and a mural and design the community poster. Will you do that for them?"

I can't help but notice he doesn't ask her to do it for him. I have a feeling as I watch Megan darting shy glances at Pete, she'd do it for him if he asked.

"It's a busy time of year," says Megan, chewing on her lower lip.

"Yeah, she's right," I add, trying to figure a way out of becoming entangled in Pete's goodie-two-shoes community rehab project.

"Four weeks, that's all I'm asking. Four weeks out of the rest of your lives. When you look at the grand scheme of things, that's not much. Plus this will mean the world to them." He makes a show of forcing us to look at the munchkins who are now racing around the room like wind-up toys and looking more like evil Chuckies than cute, adorable angel-like kids.

"Fine," says Megan, which means me playing bitch is my only option.

"Nope," I say, darting around Peter to head to the door. A part of me expects Pete to stop me, or for Megan to tell me I'm being a no-good bitch but nothing happens.

No one moves and no one stops me. I open the door and walk back down the steps feeling hollow, like I've made the biggest mistake of my life.

Shaking my head, I realize I'm wrong. The biggest mistake I made was living.

Chapter 14

Megan

My eyes feel as if they've been glued shut. Sleeping, it turns out, is something I can't do. You would think with my brother gone I'd conquer that demon. Turns out the devil lives in my head and I can't find a way to expel him. Every creak in that damn apartment had me envisioning the worst.

Hiking my backpack over my head I curse that too. The zipper broke this morning and with my luck lately that means my thermos of hot coffee is likely to fall out and smash to the ground. I am *so* in need of caffeine. I seriously thought about stopping at one of the subway stops for a brew of who knows what. However the subway was on time so I forgot about it. It's been five days since Mom went into the hospital but today she's coming home. I got up early to make sure the place was extra clean.

Johnnie insisted on playing big brother and stayed with me for four nights. They were horrible, no-sleep nights for me. We barely spoke and I'm glad he always made it a habit of sneaking into the apartment late at night. I pretended sleep and was glad he crashed in Mom's room. As usual he left a frigging mess. I noticed when I cleaned it up he made sure not to leave one personal thing of his behind. A dozen empty chip bags and beer bottles had littered our small living room, but not much else. It was like he knew his coming back home would be temporary. In a way that suits me fine. I'm also glad he took all his boxes. The hallway looks bigger and less cluttered.

Soon everything will be back to normal. I dump my coffee change into my large jar. So far in two months I've saved over thirty dollars. Then I repack my bag and head out again to make my way to the subway.

I get on the crowded subway and luck into finding a seat. I hate lugging this damn backpack but I've had to stuff my gym gear inside of it, which means the sneakers I'm wearing will have to do for today. Normally, I'd never be caught dead wearing the Salvation Army white and blue 1980's style Nikes. Today, no choice. I'm hoping no one notices but even if they do there's not much I can do about it.

I get off one line and change to another and about thirty minutes later I'm finally at the Rec center. Pushing open the orange door which is in need of a good painting, I notice two things. The place reeks of paint and that damn booming noise of Peter's has been replaced with opera. Go figure. I'd take the rap-styled Wizard of Oz music over this noise.

Slowly, I drag my feet up the steps. At the top I open the second set of orange doors. Like before it's a scene of orchestrated chaos that greets me. This time I swear to god there are a good thirty kids running around.

Peter's in the middle of the mess. He's attempting to flatten out a large roll of brown paper. It's not working. For one, the kids keep attempting to jump over it and I can tell by his voice he's getting pissed.

He looks up at me. Delight and hope radiate from those gorgeous blue eyes of his. He flashes a smile at me. My heart stutters almost to a stop. I don't need this and my body's reaction to him just angers me. The only reason I'm here in the first place is because of Lindsay's drinking episode. That's the last time I ignore the warning bells that had gone off in my head when she asked me over. I thought then it was too good to be true. Turns out I was right. It had nothing to do with becoming my friend and a lot to do with avoidance. Since I get that too, I can't find it in myself to hate her.

Peter stands up and wipes his hands on his skin tight jeans. I notice he swaggers when he walks, which emphasizes his long torso and the broad shoulders that Lindsay had laid her head on like she had a right to them.

"Okay, please help me." He flashes a wolfish grin at me, instantly melting all my hurt feelings away. With his other hand he pushes his hair off his forehead.

I dump my pack down. "Please tell me there is a pot of coffee waiting for me."

Peter laughs. "Oh yeah baby, I hear you."

Does he? I laugh because Peter's got one of those loud affectionate chuckles you either love or hate. I happen to love it. He walks me over to a small side office. The smell of dark roasted java hits my nose and I groan in pleasure.

Again Peter laughs. "I downed three before mustering my courage to face the demons."

"Why are there so many kids here today? It's Saturday. Don't they know the concept of sleeping in?" I pour myself a large cup, helping myself to two sugars and one cream. Normally, I go without the sugar but not today. It's only eight in the morning which meant my day began at six to ensure I made the hour-long trek to this damn community center on time.

He leans against an old-fashioned teacher's desk. It's got enough hard-edged graffiti on it to make it look like it belongs in the dumpster. Peter catches my look. "Bad, I know. But when you put this over it…" He pulls out a fashionable tablecloth and with one flick of his wrist the table is transformed. "Little trick I taught myself. Not everything is ugly."

Really, then what am I? I lower my eyes to my sneakers and force myself to ignore the want of all I can't have. No amount of covering or makeup can make me feel pretty.

"The kids are here every Saturday by eight. That's when I get here. Most of their parents have to work and coming here is better for them than staying home alone and getting in trouble."

I blink. Peter sounds so grown up I take a second look at him. He's only a year older than me so that makes him seventeen but trust me, most teens don't think like him. And most teens at our school wouldn't be caught dead here, so that begs the question why. Why is he doing this?

"What's up, Peter?" I ask, catching him off guard.

He blushes, making him look younger. "What do you mean?"

He knows exactly what I'm asking. I cock my head to the side and give him a pointed look. "This. Why are you doing all of this?"

He pushes off the table and moves closer to me. My heart is now officially running its own private marathon.

"I'm trying to do some good. Is that so bad?" I can tell by the way he says it he's looking for me to understand. Oh, I understand all right but I don't get it. Peter Spencer is totally loaded with enough money from his well-financed parents to buy this place. And then it hits me. The only reason he's here is something happened.

"What happened?" I wish he'd tell me but know he probably won't.

"You wouldn't believe me if I told you." He hangs his head which makes me want to reach out and touch his hair.

There is lots I wouldn't believe but then again he wouldn't believe the stuff going on in my life. That's for sure. I look down at my used sneakers and wish I had something to wear instead of yesterday's clothing. I had to get up early to make the one hour trek in to this place and since I had a pity fest happening all on my own last night, that didn't leave me time to do my laundry by hand. There's no more money for the washer and dryer machines until Mom gets her cheque next week. It's by hand or not at all.

I stare at him, wishing he'd see me for real and not the person I play at school. "Try me."

"I heard she's easy so why don't you."

Lindsay's voice whips straight through the space separating Peter and me. Peter takes a step back and I turn to confront her, the coffee sloshing around in my Styrofoam cup.

"What are you talking about?" I demand. Lindsay, as usual looks like a million bucks. The envious demon inside of me hates her.

She's wearing blood red colored boots you just know are made with real Italian leather. They slide up past her knees to cover black tights. She's got a designer black off-the-shoulder top with the word 'Nice' outlined in gold layering on one side of the shirt, which ties at the bottom past her hip. Real gold hooped earrings grace her lobes and she's got a matching red purse. She looks like she's dressed for a club, not a rec center.

She places her hands on her hips to give me one of her you-are-so-dirt stares.

"Rebecca said she saw you get in a car with a guy who is known for doing girls. Some type of low life."

Shit. Rebecca saw me and my brother, Johnnie together. No frigging way. And if she did, what the hell was she doing in that neighborhood, meaning my neighborhood. Worse, what does that mean doing girls? I long to ask, but the only thing I plead is mistaken identity.

"Think again. Wasn't me." Lying through my teeth isn't knew for me.

"You sure, because she certainly nailed down your clothing, which come to think of, it is exactly what you're wearing today."

That hurts. "You are so wasting your time." I slide past her. I'd rather deal with the ugly munchkins than Ms. Prissy Perfect.

"Stop being a bitch," says Peter.

I can't believe he stood up for me.

"I need both of you to get along so can it Lindsay. Megan," yells Peter, like I've managed to move half way across the gym floor or something. Now I know why he stood up for me. He needs me to deal with the mess of kids who are almost bouncing off the walls. "If you can get that long paper rolled out and get some of the kids to help with the mural, we'll be all set."

I glance at him, wishing I didn't notice how close he's standing to Lindsay. Or how perfect they look together.

"Fine, what do you want painted?" I decide if I can tackle this asap I might make it out early. Since I've got a good thirty minute subway ride to my reserve unit the latest I can stay is noon. Today is a mandatory training day. That means lots of jogging, pushups, and marching, so gym gear is the norm. I glance at my backpack and can't help but notice the zipper's down more, like someone was peeking at my stuff. Probably looking to see if I had anything they could swipe. No such luck with my stash. I smile, make my way over to the massive roll of paper and recruit two girls who look like they want to help.

"You hold that end and together we'll get it straight." I urge them each to one side. It takes us only a few minutes before we've got the paper flat and straight.

Peter pops over to tell me where the paints are and my recruits follow me eagerly to the janitorial room. The three of us start to bring out the materials we will need and within seconds I've got a group of a dozen kids looking at me with eager eyes.

"What exactly did you want us to paint, Peter?"

I yell at him because he's now deep in a conversation with Lindsay, who I notice is tapping her designer foot like she'd rather be anywhere else than here. I get that, but unlike her that applies to most places I go.

Peter leaves Lindsay, giving a shake to his head as he walks over to me. He bends down to my level. "The theme is the Wizard of Oz meets Santa…so anything along those lines will do. We'll probably need three large murals because we change the set three times. And Lindsay can be a bitch sometimes, so don't let it get to you. That's just how she is."

Wow, Peter called Lindsay a bitch. Somehow I don't think he means the word like it's supposed to mean.

I finish off my now cold coffee. "She's wrong, it wasn't me." I have no idea why I feel the need to say that to him, but I don't want him getting the wrong impression. Not that the right impression is something I can let him figure out either.

Peter smiles at me, causing my stomach to get that butterfly feeling. "I know. It doesn't matter. I'm really happy you're both here."

"Yeah, I get that, so you want to tell me why you're really doing this?" I make a point to force myself to look at him.

I see the wall go up so fast in his expression it startles me.

"I'm doing good," he says, like that explains everything—him in charge of the anti-drug committee at school and now this—the rich kid doing good for the poor. Maybe it does explain things. Maybe not. That's the thing—since more than half of my day is spent in a lie, the truth has become harder and harder to decipher.

A part of me wonders if this is his pity project. I find myself watching how Peter acts around the kids and I realize that's not true. Peter is different here. I can't put my finger on it but he seems more real.

I shrug, turning my attention to the kids who are waiting for my instructions. "When you want to tell me for real your reasons I promise to understand."

He gives a hurtful laugh and straightens up. "I highly doubt that."

The way he says it hits me. Truth. Straight-up.

"Try me," I repeat, wishing he would in more ways than one.

Chapter 15

Lindsay

"To get them to respect me I have to dress the part." I have no idea why I'm explaining myself to Peter. Doesn't he get the whole Paula Abdul thingy? I quirk my eyebrows up at him and place my hands on my hips for a dramatic show, enjoying the feel of my new purse swinging from my covered up wrist. You don't have to be a professional to play one and trust me, I've got play acting down to a science.

The noise from the kids is driving me nuts and I've only been here for fifteen minutes. The thought of spending my entire Saturday morning here is daunting. Not that I have anything else to do.

"Okay, tell me who you've picked for the play." I force Peter to turn his attention back to me instead of Megan. God, I can't believe she's wearing the same clothes she had on yesterday. Is she out of her freaking mind? And when Rebecca called me last night to dish the dirt on her I had thought she was nuts. Seeing her and Peter flirting and realizing Rebecca had been correct makes me wonder if she's set her sights on Peter. She can have him. What kills me are the lies. Who is Megan really?

I wonder if she, like me, fakes it. Not that I care. I force myself to pay attention to Peter's list of kids he's picked for this god awful play.

"Look, write their names down for me and I'll work with that." He instantly follows my command. See, looking the part pays off.

Armed now with my list, I call out the kids' names. Thirteen kids line up in front of me. Each of them looks at me like I'm a queen. I purse my lips together and for the first time I feel nervous. What the hell am I doing? I don't know anything about acting.

Like Peter reads my mind, he walks over and damn if he doesn't say something insightful. "You will be great. I trust you."

Really, I don't trust myself.

An hour later I'm totally impressed with myself. I think my favorite kid is this little girl with a riot of tight black curls framing her small brown face. Her name's Ashanti and she's got the voice of a diva. For a ten year-old kid she's following my advice like I'm a super star. My next favorite is George. George isn't the lead in the play. He's the cowardly lion who Peter has dressed in a Santa suit. He's tall, lanky and perfect for the role with his carrot-hued hair and freckle face. He keeps stumbling over his size ten shoes. God, his mom must hate buying him sneakers. He's from Russia and has the most adorable accent I've ever heard on a twelve year-old. Then there's Kyra, Mylan, Sou, and Eli who were made to be helpers. They are my eager beaver team. I can't help laugh at something Sou says to Kyra. Sou, who is nine, is the most precocious kid I've ever met. She puts me to shame. Kyra is painfully shy, but you can tell Sou is like her big sister. The rest of my ensemble of kids I've put to work on their dance moves. They seriously need to get it together.

Peter hands me a cup of tea. "How many weeks did you say we had?" I tried the coffee but my run to the washroom wasn't pleasant. My constant nausea is killing me. Worse, the smell of Peter's cologne is like a freaking puke button for me.

Mustering my courage, I take a sip. "Peter don't take this the wrong way or anything but I've become very sensitive to smell lately and your cologne is killing me."

He laughs at me and I instantly feel better. "We've got three weeks to get the kids ready for their debut and thanks for the warning. I watched you run to the bathroom to puke your guts out earlier. Wondered if you might have hit the liquor again?"

Don't I wish. "Nope. Think I'm coming down with something." Something I seriously don't want. I can't help notice his cheeks are flushed. Damn, I've embarrassed him. Before he turns away to check in on Megan's set design, he leans in closer.

"After today no more cologne. I'll be au naturelle." He turns, but not before giving me a friendly wink. The thought of Peter au naturelle is kind of gross. I mean he's cute and all, but the thought of any guy naked is not on my wish list.

"Thanks." I take another tentative sip of the hot tea, waiting for that feeling of bile to rise. When it doesn't happen I start drinking the tea in earnest.

By the time I've finished half the tea I'm starting to feel more normal. The roll of nausea has settled and the smell of the paints Megan's working with isn't as obnoxious. By the time twelve comes around for our lunch break, I find myself telling Peter I'll stay for another hour or so to help the kids work on their dance moves. I might as well. The only person at home today is Greg. As usual Mom had to dart off to a conference. She promised me she'd be back tonight, so at least I don't have to worry about that other shit.

"How was your day?"

I ignore Greg's attempt at civility. Instead I march upstairs to my room and shut the door. A few minutes later I hear the front door open and close and the sound of his sports car zooming away. I don't realize I'm holding my breath until I feel my muscles relax. God I hate him. It's six o'clock. I stayed at the rec center way longer than anticipated. Megan left around noon promising she'd be back Monday night to help but we didn't talk. I wanted to talk to her but after the way I acted in the morning I get why she shunned me. If I was in her shoes I'd do the same. Being a bitch can be lonely.

Changing into my comfy flannel pj's I head back downstairs. I make sure the front door is locked and then head to the kitchen to find something to eat. If I eat another piece of pizza I'm going to be sick forever. Knowing my stomach is sensitive I go for the chicken noodle soup. Plus it's easy to heat up and I'm starved. A minute later, I head back up to my room with my bowl. Flipping open my laptop I turn it on. My cell's buzzing away and when I pick it up I've missed the caller. It's a message from Rebecca. I ignore it. She just wants to know where I was all day. Like I'm about to confess that to her. No way. I would become the laughing stock of the school if anyone found out I spent my Saturday helping kids at a rec center. But, doing that felt real and for the first time since I moved here, today felt good. And, in a weird way, meaningful.

I manage to eat all the soup. I ditch doing my pile of homework and put it off until tomorrow. I'm tired so I flick on a movie on my computer and settle down to watch it on my bed.

I must have fallen asleep. When I wake up, my computer's not on the bed but I instantly tense when I feel a hand slide around my middle to snake underneath my pj shirt.

"Get out." I grind the words out through my shaking teeth.

The stench of stale beer hits me and I have to fight not to puke in my bed. Greg ignores me, as usual.

"Get out. Or I'll scream." This time I mean it.

Even though he's drunk my words penetrate. He gives an evil chuckle, sliding his hand up further to paw my breast. I'm shaking so much now I know there are tears leaking from my eyes. None of that will stop him.

"Scream all you want. You like it. I know it. And your mom's not home."

His words hit me and I realize he's telling the truth. When I was younger he'd come in to paw me when my mother was home. I was too frightened then to say or do anything about it. Then when things progressed and he raped me, it was too late to tell Mom. In fact Greg taunted me for months to tell her, also letting me know my mother would choose him over me in a heartbeat. I didn't want to believe him and when things finally got too much for me I finally spoke up. A lot of good that did me!

He attempts to climb on top of me. I twist underneath him like a cornered snake. One of his hands holds my shoulder down. Thank god I'm wearing my pj set. If I had on a nightie, kicking him wouldn't help. Tonight it does. He pushes down on my shoulder hard, pinning me in place. I'll probably end up with bruises on my shoulder from his fingers that are digging into my skin but I don't care. Forcibly, I turn my head into my pillow.

I take all the hurtful words he spits at me. Whore. Cunt. Fucking slut. That's about the extent of Greg's repertoire. Thank god. I've heard those same words for over two years. At one time they shocked me. Not anymore. He says them more to justify his actions not understanding I've associated them with him and not me. I feel myself start to distance myself when his hand slides inside my panties. I want to fight but my experience with Greg is he likes it the more I struggle, and trust me the bruising and pain I get aren't worth it.

Something clicks off in my brain. I'm lying there in the dark in my bedroom filled with my stuff. I notice I've left the door to my closet open and I see one of my new shirts has slipped off its hanger. There aren't any pictures hanging on my walls. Why bother? I don't want to remember anything about this room. I hear grunts, shuffles and feel my panties being yanked down. They are bunched up around my ankles. Not that it matters. Greg's heavy weight, the smell of beer and his cologne add to my torture. He attempts to kiss me, but my head is pushed so far into my pillow I'm hoping to suffocate myself. There's lots of grunting on Greg's part, along with a slew of more curses. My body's gone limp in disgust and I've removed myself from the scene.

With my eyes shut I see my favorite tree that used to be in our backyard in Halifax. Tonight I've climbed it. I'm really high up, but I'm not worried about the branch breaking. No matter my weight, this tree will always hold me. It's that conviction and escapism enabling me to breathe through my living nightmare. I feel the cool salty air coming off the harbor. The stars are shining and whenever I visit my special tree it's a perfect half-moon. I like that. I like how the moon looks like a pizza pocket and that's how I get through it.

When Greg's done, I don't move. He scrambles out of the bed and I hear him adjust his clothes. He tells me I'm a cock tease, whore and mother fucking slut. As usual I don't respond. I lie there still snug in my tree, waiting for the stench of him to leave. He throws the duvet cover over me. I didn't realize it had slipped free from the assault. I don't make a move to adjust it. Only when he finally stumbles from my room, when I hear the bedroom door click shut, do I turn my head to my pillow and scream until my throat's burning raw, until the tears I've held in check can't flow anymore. Then I get up, throwing off the duvet and head to the bathroom.

I lean over the white toilet seat and grip the sides of it. My body's shaking and I can feel Greg's semen sliding down the insides of my thighs. I fall to the floor, barely keeping my head above the rim of the toilet. I notice the small lines on my wrists, the tiny stitched-up incisions that remind me I tried to get out of this mess and that it didn't work.

Just when I want to throw up I can't. I do the only thing I can think of. I stick my finger down my throat until my gag reflex works in earnest and finally I release all my emotions straight into the toilet. I'm not sure how long I repeat the process but it's only when my stomach muscles start to cramp and yellowish brown bile has filled the toilet that I stop. Weakly, I turn on the shower. I make sure it's scalding hot water before I step inside the stall. The spray hits my skin, burning me, but I stand there, taking it. I pick up the soap and start to scrub away the filth. I repeat my actions three times.

By the time I'm done my skin looks like an overcooked lobster. Turning off the shower I step out, not feeling any cleaner. There's a lot of hate coursing through me. A lot of 'why me' but at that moment, when I'm holding my pink razor with longing in my hand, I'm thinking, *Damn you Mother. You lied.*

Chapter 16

Megan

Monday is finally here and I'm glad. It's hard being home with Mom. It's just the two of us. She asked once about Johnnie. I told her what she wanted to hear. He came to visit, he's fine, and yes he's working somewhere. That was it. I didn't tell her what happened to me. Or what happened between Johnnie and me to end our friendly brotherly-sisterly relationship. She doesn't need that.

Mom looks fragile, like the bump to her head knocked a bit of the fight out of her. That scares me. She's always been the positive one. I know it's more a show for me but I didn't realize how much I needed it until two days later she's still lying in bed. It's like she can't be bothered to waste the effort to get up. That's not like my mom.

A community nurse came in on Sunday to check up on her. She was nice, but I didn't like her appraising looks. She told me my mom had a bad concussion and said how she's feeling is normal. I wanted to shout at her that there is no normal. My mom has MS and not one day to the next is the same in her life. I bit my lip and nodded, anxiously wanting her to leave.

Only when people come to our apartment do I notice how we must look to them. I'm glad at least Johnnie took his boxes, but still there's no mistaking the odor of poverty or sickness. I didn't offer her anything to eat. We don't have anything. Oh, I've got the cash, thanks to Johnnie, who left a hundred dollars in twenties on my dresser. I won't spend a penny of it. Using his cash feels dirty, like he's attempting to buy back my sisterly love. Not sure I'm capable of ever giving him that trust again. He might be family but we act more like strangers than family now.

There's a jar of no-name peanut butter, and our usual—a box of saltines. Such a lovely meal. The only benefit is I won't get fat.

And being overweight at my school is worse than failing a class.

I smell more than see Lindsay coming closer. Her expensive French perfume smells like the perfect mixture of lilacs and fresh daisies. Part of me is anxious and part of me is envious. I wonder if she's going to ridicule me again or worse, ignore me. Maybe I should ignore her. I certainly went out of my way to do that on Saturday but I think it hurt me more than her. It's not in me to be intentionally mean. No, that's more Lindsay's style.

Feigning interest in my locker, I attempt to ignore her, but she walks up to where my locker is located. I'm hyper aware of what's happening in the hallway, which is a lot of public displays of affection. The girls with boyfriends like to flaunt it and the boys love it. I guess there are some universal things that are the same for all schools.

Lindsay leans back against the bank of lockers, looking outward at the crowd of girls milling around. She doesn't say anything to me. Instead she opens her designer purse. It's different than the one she wore yesterday. Another stab of jealousy ripples through me.

"You're not going to tell anyone where we were yesterday, are you?"

Is she freaking nuts? "Please. Adding to my list of sins, no thank you."

She breathes a sigh of relief. I get that.

She kicks off from the locker wall and stands next to me. "That's great. So see you tonight."

I must be hallucinating, or maybe my peanut butter and cracker diet is affecting me in more ways than one. It actually sounded to me like Lindsay's looking forward to tonight. I can tell you I'm certainly not. Lindsay hasn't moved. What gives?

"Yeah, I'll be there. Late but there." I shut my locker and turn away from her and start walking to class. Lindsay follows me. This isn't like her. Normally she'd cross the space in the hall to ensure she wasn't close to me. She waves at Rebecca who as usual is lip-locked to Blair. I shudder. Just once I wish they'd get caught in the act. Then again, knowing how loaded Rebecca's parents are it probably wouldn't matter for her. Me, on the other hand, oh yeah, I'd find myself flat on my ass the minute I tried to break the rules. Money rules this school and it's not something I can ever forget.

As we walk, side by side, but not chatting or attempting to look at each other, I can't help noticing Lindsay's twisting another new bracelet around her right wrist. I swear to god the bracelets get larger and more expensive each week.

She catches my eye and a tired smile flits across her face.

"Mom's gift."

Like that explains it all. Must be nice, I think, wishing once my mom could afford a gift for me. Then I think of Mom at home alone and probably still in bed and I feel guilty. I'm glad I asked our next door neighbor, Mrs. Burrows to pop over to visit her. I also gave her the phone number of the school in case there's another emergency. She looked at the number and I know she wanted to ask me a few questions but me having to rush off to catch the subway saved me. The less people in our building who know where I go to school, the better. While two of my used-to-be-friends live on the top floor, they haven't said even boo to me since I told them. I'm glad they haven't egged our windows. A laugh flies out of me, startling me and Lindsay.

"What's so funny?" Lindsay turns to look at me, forcing me to stop.

I'm laughing because the notion of anyone in our building wasting food, like eggs, to smash on windows is so funny it's sad. We don't waste food in my neighborhood. Wasting people, well that's an entirely different thing. "Nothing. You wouldn't understand." I try to brush past her.

"I didn't mean what I said the other day," says Lindsay.

For a moment I'm stunned stupid. I freeze to the spot, feeling heat surface on my face. I don't want to talk about what she said. Especially not here.

Lindsay's rushing on with words in a hushed whisper. I feel people watching, listening to us and I get more nervous.

"You didn't, did you? I just know Rebecca's wrong," she says.

I can tell by how's she looking at me she's wanting the juicy gossip and not the godawful truth. There it is. The lie she wants to hear from me. Holding my laptop closer to my rapidly rising chest, I inch closer to her. "Not everything is black and white, Lindsay."

This time she laughs. You can tell by the harshness of her chuckle she's not thinking of anything funny.

"Trust me I live in a world of gray, so I get that. It's just that I wondered…" She looks down at the overly polished marble floor. "Do you want it?"

Want it? We're talking in a coded language about sex, I think. Here in the hall of our school where teachers roam while the students pass us without a care in the world. This is so not the place for this discussion but I don't ever want to talk about this.

"This conversation is over." I hiss my words at her. I turn around, and this time when she says something that shocks me I force myself to continue on to class. However her words haunt me all through math and I wish for once I had been late for school. Instead I repeat her words over and over again in my head trying to figure out what she meant by them.

"Sometimes I want that blackness so much I can't think straight," she had said.

It dawns on me during Religion class. Lindsay wasn't talking about sex. She was talking about death. The longing in her voice rings louder than the damn bell for lunch.

The bigger question is what would make a spoiled rich girl who has everything she wants at her fingertips to die. I vow to find out tonight. Friend or frenemy I need to know the answer.

It's my turn in the confessional. My legs move automatically but my mind's thinking of what I can say to the priest.

"My dear, is there anything you would like to confess?"

Oh, there's a list of things I want to confess but telling is not going to happen. I've had faith slammed down my throat since I was born. The whole nine yards of being Catholic. Sunday school, Mom gifting me with my own rosary, getting baptized and weekly confessionals. I lied at my first confessional and haven't stopped. Honestly, I think everyone in this school lies to Father Donahue.

"Father, please forgive me for I have sinned. I cursed at my mom," I say, with practiced ease.

His answering silence is my cue he's waiting for more. He always does. I envision him licking his lips and rubbing his sweaty hands with glee, just waiting for my lies.

"My child it is good for the heart for you to confess to God."

Yeah, right. This might be good for his heart and position in the school but that's it. I gave up on God when I learned for real what MS meant for my mom. For years she tried to make light of it, but by the time I was seven the wheelchair became her life.

Then it became migraines, pills that knocked her out for days on end and a list of other ailments that no amount of praying cured.

"Well, Father, I touched myself."

"Yes, my child," he urges me on.

This performance could make me a super star. By the time I'm done outlining what I did to myself, I have my punishment. Ten hail Mary's and I must spend an hour this week in silent prayer and reflection on my deeds. Sure, not a problem. Not like I've got a social life waiting for me at lunch or something.

I exit the confessional and bump into Lindsay. We mumble apologies. I wonder what she's going to tell the Priest. My hunch is she'll lie like me. The truth always hurts like hell so why tell.

Chapter 17

Lindsay

I am soaked to the bone. Next time I'm taking Peter's offer of a lift earlier. Instead I ignored him for a bit but a block later after the torrential rain came I didn't hesitate when he pulled his car to the curb and let me crawl dripping wet inside. He laughed. I didn't think it was funny. I yell my thanks and promise once again to be at the rec center after supper. I dart inside. My hot red super wide-collared sweater is totally ruined. Dumping my gear by the side of the stairs I hear laughter.

Thank god, my mother's home. The closer I get to the voices I realize it's not just my mother. When I step into the kitchen I inwardly groan. Not another renovation. My plea is obviously ignored when Mother-dearest introduces Ms. Linda Catcher. Going on automatic, I shake the lady's hand, gaining a pointed look from my mother. Dripping on her floors is a big no-no. Too bad. I'm soaked. My long hair is drenched and the ends of it are freezing my back.

When I see Greg and Mother start their adorable oh-so-lovey-dovey couple routine I wonder if Ms. Catcher notices how fake it is. Greg's got his arm drawn tight around my mother's mid-section, but his eyes are looking hungrily at Ms. Catcher. She's certainly his type: blonde, obviously wealthy and you can tell by how she's looking at him she likes how he looks.

My mother unlocks herself from Greg to move closer to me. I tense. She had better not try to pull a hug from me. I hate when she does that. At one time I used to give her tight oh-so-appreciated hugs every time she came home on time. When coming home on time stopped and when she started staying away longer, leaving me with nanny after nanny, the hugs stopped.

"Linda is showing us what we can do with our kitchen. This is so outdated," says Mother, sliding past me to pour three glasses of red wine. Greg gives her a kiss when she hands him his wine. The two of them make me sick.

Ms. Catcher drones on about what's so outdated in our kitchen. I roll my eyes, earning a harsh look from Mother who thinks she watches me like a hawk when she's home. If she really watched she'd know what was going on in this constant reno-home.

According to the real estate agent who showed us this house the kitchen was recently redesigned. However, none of that matters. My mother's into getting the best and most expensive things she can. Her goal is to impress the people who visit. After all, when you're stuck with a not-so-perfect daughter, the next best thing, beside Greg who is her stud-candy, are expensive useless things. Things that mean nothing to her. She's never home long enough for them to matter.

I find myself nodding at whatever Ms. Catcher is saying. Usually the nod is a good move when you're not paying attention but obviously not when mother claps her hands with glee. *Shit, what did I just do?*

"Darling, you don't know how long I've waited for you to say yes to that."

Mother's statement hits me. The one thing she's hounded me about since moving into this mega-mansion is my room. She wanted to hire a designer from the get-go, but honestly, I like my bedroom. It's definitely bare by my mother's standards and there's nothing personal hanging from my walls, but that suits me fine. I'm pretty sure Megan thought it was great, but my mother hates it. I love it. End of story.

"Sorry, I missed something," I say.

Mother's lips purse together, and her brown beetle-colored eyes drill into me. I force myself not to move when she edges closer, almost touching but not quite. "Greg's my witness. You nodded your head when Linda suggested we redo your bedroom and we really must."

"No. We really mustn't." I put as much sauce into that statement as I can without earning a lecture later on.

"Must not," she corrects. By her tone I know I'm not going to win this argument.

"Leave it, Mel. It's Linds' room and it's up to her, not you. Plus we're going to be busy with our things, sweetie-pie."

Barf. Gag. Kill me while I stand here having to be forced to listen to this drabble of shit. My mother's real name is Melissa, but she ditched that about a decade ago when she realized the men in the boardrooms took her more seriously when she went by Mel. She told me if she could rename me she'd go with something unisex, like Jamie.

Then it dawns on me, Greg is coming to my rescue. My eyes narrow. What the hell does he want?

"But Gregster, it won't take long for Linds' room to be done, will it?" asks Mother to Ms. Catcher, who like me you can tell is slightly nauseated with the syrupy talk.

If she thinks that's bad I know first-hand it's nothing. Whenever Mother throws one of her parties, the two of them act like they haven't seen each other in days, with their hands all over each other and apple-pie sweet talk. It's enough to make anyone hurl or wish she'd offered up hashish baked brownies. That at least might make it funny.

"Sweetie-pie the only room left is next to ours and we wouldn't want Linds to hear…"

He gives a fake smile at Mother and winks at her. It dawns on me then. Moving closer would cramp his style.

"Actually, Mother, I think you're right. It's about time I had my room redesigned to better suit me." I force back my shoulders, and flash one of my thank you smiles at everyone. It's a look I've logged many hours in the mirror to perfect.

I can tell by Mother's posture she's thrilled I agreed. I can tell by Greg's silence he's not. That suits me fine.

"Why don't I go change and then I can show Ms. Catcher my room. I'd love to go through some designer books with you." Not really, but the game has been set.

Mother leans over and gives me a peck on my cheek like I've just aced a test. If she knew my real reason she'd give me an F.

Two hours later I'm at the rec center. I pleaded study group at the library and as usual it was no questions asked. The minute I walk in Peter's on me.

"Now, don't freak out when you see Ashanti."

"What?" I ask, not understanding. But before he can say anything else, in walks Megan.

Peter grabs both of us and hauls us into his side office. "Both of you, don't freak out when you see Ashanti. Things like this happen and it's best if we just go on, pretend it's okay."

I glance at Megan. I can tell she understands what he's saying but this time I'm not nodding. "I don't get it. What happened to her?"

Megan gives a humorless laugh. "I'm betting she got beaten, right?" She looks at Peter who gives a slow nod.

"She'll tell you she fell and landed on one of her brother's toys the wrong way."

Megan shrugs like none of this is new to her.

"Wait a sec, are you saying her father beat her?"

Megan dumps her large backpack on Peter's chair. "Or her mother. Doesn't matter. A beating's a beating."

Part of me can't believe she sounds so nonchalant. Ashanti's only a kid. Wait a sec, wasn't I a child when Greg stumbled into my room and raped me? I close my eyes and fight for a breath as that night flashes hot and vivid through me. My stomach rolls and the taste of blood and bile fills my throat.

"You okay?" asks Peter.

I'm not, but he can't help. I take a seat on one of the worn chairs and force myself to ignore the truth of my situation. What's wrong with me isn't an easy fix. "Is she okay?" I ask, ignoring his inquiry of my health.

"Bruised up, but she'll be fine by the time we debut. Don't worry about that."

Megan tisks. I'm wondering if she's thinking my thoughts. I wasn't worried if Ashanti could perform, I was worried more about her. Megan's about to say something else when one of the younger girls comes in and informs us that Ashanti's crying in the corner.

"I'll handle this," says Megan, before either Peter or I can step forward.

Peter and I share a confused look. Shy, mousy Megan is coming out of her shell it seems. Just when did her take charge attitude blossom? Probably about the time we got blackmailed into coming here.

Peter runs a hand through his hair and looks at me. "Do you think I should talk to her?"

"Are you nuts? You don't know anything about kids," I try to make light of this dark situation and fail.

"And neither do you. Guess it's good Megan went. She must have siblings or something. She looked like she knew exactly what to do."

I have no idea if Megan has siblings. She mentioned her father had died and it was her and her mother but I never asked anything else about her life. I tend not to ask a lot of questions because I don't want people prying into my so-called perfect life.

Too many questions and I might slip up and tell the truth for a change. Now, wouldn't that be a shit disturbing mistake.

Twenty minutes later Ashanti is composed and reciting her lines like a pro. I'm trying hard not to stare. Her right eye is swollen and part of her cheek is a nasty purplish color. Toy my ass! Her face has fist stamped all over it.

Megan sidles up to me when Ashanti's done her part. George is moving to center stage to play the stumbling cowardly lion. The role is perfect for him.

"She'll be okay. Just don't say anything to her. She's kind of emotional about it."

"Shouldn't someone call social services or something?" I whisper the words, not wanting the kids milling around us to overhear our conversation.

Megan snorts. "Yeah, like that's going to do any good." I can tell by the way Megan says it she means it. I'm really naive because I thought social services did good.

I tap my foot in time to the Christmas jingle Peter's cranked up, and hate the fact I'm starting to like being here. "I disagree with you. She shouldn't go home to that."

"No, that's right. She should go into the system so someone she doesn't know can play punching bag with her, or better yet molest her. Yeah, that's such a great idea."

I blink and look at Megan. "Are you for real?"

"Sadly, Lindsay that is real. Trust me, the system won't work for Ashanti."

I turn on her, grab her arm and move us away from the kids nearby. "Megan, this is serious shit. She can't go home."

Megan gives her arm a shake. "Lindsay, you don't get it. That's really the reality for these kids and many more like them. They deal with serious stuff all the time. She'll be okay."

"What gives Megan? Just how do you know she'll be worse

off?"

Megan's staring at me. "Trust me, I know. Not all of us live your perfect life."

There it is. The lie that binds me tighter than a friendship bracelet. I don't have a perfect life by any stretch of the imagination but I'm so caught up in playing my role I can't ad lib.

She darts past me before I can ask more questions. My first question was going to be, what the hell happened to you? However, since she might turn that question back at me, I'm glad I bit my lip and shut up.

Chapter 18

Megan

The collage the kids and I worked on looks great. I try not to watch Ashanti, skipping across center stage, but fail miserably. I get where Lindsay's coming from. She wants to save the kids from the ugliness of their reality. Going into the system won't save her. I know that first hand.

My eyes have a will of their own. They keep following Peter. He's a walking, talking contradiction. At school Peter's got wealth stamped all over him and he likes to flaunt it. Here, he's relaxed and from the expression on his face I know he likes working with these kids. This is not a hobby to him. It might have started out like that but I would bet Lindsay's flashy new boots, coming here means a lot to Peter.

"You aren't still thinking about Ashanti?"

Peter hands me the tin can with the five clean paintbrushes. I had meant to clean the brushes after the kids and I finished painting our first scene, but I ended up getting caught up in my candid conversation with Lindsay.

"What happened to her is wrong. Plain and simple. But the world is filled with ugliness. I'm not surprised by it. Like I told Lindsay I'm not sure telling anyone would do any good." Squatting, I reach out and start to lay out the paint brushes. The kids are having a twenty minute break but I want my five star artists to come back ready to work.

Peter kneels down beside me and I try not to notice how close he is. My heart's beating extra fast because I get nervous when he's real close.

"When I first came here…when something like this happened the first time, my supervisor took me into her office. She told me to have a seat and explained in vivid detail where to draw the line. Broken bones and sexual abuse get reported. A slap here or there, ignore."

If he's waiting for me to gasp in outrage, he's got the wrong girl.

"Wait a sec, you had a supervisor? Where is she now?"

"Fired because of budget cuts two weeks later. If I didn't come here there would be no one to supervise these kids. The place would be forced to shut down."

He leans closer and wipes his hands on his skin-tight jeans. I'm reciting the lines to Katy Perry's Teenage Dream song in my head and totally get those lyrics now.

"You handled things really well. I think there's more to Megan than Megan lets on."

Keeping my eyes glued to that damn brown paper is the hardest thing. "Peter, I don't understand you. Why are you doing all of this? You don't need to be here."

"Yeah, Megan, I do. At first when I started here I didn't like it much. Kind of cramped my style, but it only took two days for my eyes to be opened. I can't explain it, but I want to be here. Things matter. Plus it beats the hell out of hanging around the hospital." He gives a soft chuckle, like he knows he's let the cat out of the bag.

I'm so glad that Peter doesn't bring up our hospital run in. I'm not interested in rehashing any of that. I'd take this place any day over the hospital.

"Wow, that's profound. I don't know Peter, the coffee was pretty damn good at that cafeteria," I say, forcing myself to chuckle.

Our arms accidentally touch and I feel that contact all the way to my squished in toes. I need a new pair of sneakers, but unless a twenty dollar bill arrives miraculously from the air, and the Salvation Army has my nine-and-a-half shoe size, squished toes will have to do.

Eyes down…eyes down…eyes down. My mantra doesn't help and I find my head moving up so I can look at him. His blue eyes search my face. I'm not sure what he sees but I'm hoping it's not the new zit I feel forming along my chin.

"So explain to me again why you and Lindsay are fighting?" he asks, catching me off guard both with his heated look and switch in conversation.

I get up and brush my hands on my jeans. "It's complicated, but basically she used me and pretended to be my friend when she's really my frenemy."

He nods, like that's what he had figured out. Probably everyone at school assumes the same thing.

"You know what I think," he says, standing very close to me.

I nod, willing him to go on.

"I think you're good for her. It can't be easy moving away from all you know to come here."

Yeah, he's got that right. Wait a sec, he's not talking about me. He's talking about Lindsay.

I attempt to move away from him. I need space, because I can't stand it when Peter comes to Lindsay's rescue. No one ever saves me, but they all want to jump on board to save the spoiled rich girl. "Yeah, well that doesn't explain how she's treated me."

"No you're right, Megan, but like you, I think Lindsay could use a real friend."

"She's got Rebecca, so she'll be fine."

Peter laughs, causing Lindsay to turn her head and finally notice us. I wonder if she'll march over and demand to find out what's so funny. Instead, she moves closer to the stage and ignores us.

"Like I was saying, she could use a real friend."

Before I can think of something witty to say, we get bombarded by the rush of kids who plow through the door from the outside. Peter's words cling like sticky tack to me for the rest of the morning.

Personal experience tells me to keep my mouth shut and as hard as that is, I manage to get through the rest of the morning pretending to ignore Lindsay when I'm super aware of everything she's doing. I just wish she'd see me…the real me and even though she says she doesn't believe Rebecca I know deep down she doesn't trust me. She apologized but the words rang hollow. I don't want to believe in her. Everyone I've believed in has disappointed me.

Sad because she seems to be really connecting with the kids. She's doing great. Why does that make me feel guilty for treating her like shit all morning?

Chapter 19

Lindsay

Well into week one of my bedroom renovation and I'm trying hard to keep it together. What the hell was I thinking? Oh, I know, anything to cramp Greg's style. Unfortunately, it's also cramping mine.

The bedroom next to my mother's is large but she's had her decorator do it up. Honestly, it's so not my style. Dark prints, a velvet red bedspread and large art vogue prints she thinks are fashionable hang on the walls. It's something straight out of a Vanity Fair magazine attempting to do a special on the Elizabethan age—downright gaudy.

"Liking your new room, Linds?"

"Get lost." I don't bother to turn around. Instead I try my usual route—ignore Greg.

He walks into my room, flips over my freaking hair brush and I can tell he's wanting to talk. I never want to talk to him. Ever.

Mother's home. The slam of the back door is the dead giveaway. Hallelujah. Saved by my mother, for once.

"You might want to get out now." Walking past Greg to go into my adjoining bathroom, I try not to shiver in disgust. The ultra-modern décor in the washroom, with the standing only see-through shower makes my skin crawl.

Greg grabs my arm, pulling me back into my room. I bite my lip from crying out.

"You think I don't know your game," he says.

I visualize my mother's routine. She's yanking off her high-heeled boots, hanging up her coat, checking her Blackberry's email and ensuring it's plugged in on the side hall table. I yank my arm out of his hold and the urge to scream my head off at him sails through me. I bank that idea though. Not like Mother can save me from this situation.

"Fuck you Greg."

He looks at me, long and hard. I know he wants to say something to me, but he also is tuned into Mother's habits. Two more minutes and her feet will hit the stairs.

"We're not done you and me. This is only temporary."

I'm wishing I had super hero powers. Something like the ability to shoot fire from my eyes would come in handy now. Since I don't have that I simply glare at him with my 'you are so dog-shit' look I've mastered.

Mother's climbing the stairs now. Her steps are always loud. There's nothing soft about my mother—from her tread to her treatment of me. She's got a reputation as a shark when it comes to business and she's a piranha when it comes to Greg getting remotely close to me. Jealousy is hard-wired into her. And, no amount of telling her I'm not into Greg one bit helps. Since Greg likes to foster Mother's inferiority complex I want him gone from my room pronto.

"Leave Greg. Now."

"Only if you say please."

I blink. This is how Greg works. My heart's beating that slow thud like a basketball let loose in a court. Just let me go. That's not going to happen. My mouth feels like it's full of sour candies but I spit it out. "Please leave."

He grins. That's the thing with Greg. He likes to push me when he knows it pisses me off.

"I know you want me just as much as I want you. I'm into your game," says Greg, leaning his body closer to mine. I shake my head at him. There's no point arguing with him.

He's got a minute before she's at the top of the landing.

I get no satisfaction when he finally leaves my room.

"Darling, what took you so long?" Greg reaches out to pull my mother into a hug. She giggles, looking at me standing still in my room. It's a questionable look. I'm all into making her feel uncomfortable.

"Linds had a problem with her shade, so I yanked it down for her."

I can't help glance at said shade. Damn, I had hoped he'd get caught in a lie. The shade is down and it's up to me to pretend there's truth in what he said.

"Yup." That's all I can manage. Anything else and I'm seriously going to gag.

* * *

On Wednesday I've decided my new hate is Biology class. For starters we have a new teacher who has obviously been kept in the dark that my mother made a generous donation to our new downtown campus because he hates me. That's got to be it. Why else would he team me up with Megan? I know she's as shocked as me that he re-arranged the lab partners we had picked out on Monday. To top that off we're dissecting a frog.

My deli sandwich wants freedom from my stomach and it's taking all my tummy muscles to keep that under control. Or in my case keep it down.

"This is just gross."

Nice to know Megan echoes my thoughts.

"Totally." I hope she'll be the one to make the initial incision. That damn frog has been lying on our slab for a good five minutes and there is no way I'm cutting into it.

Mr. Snaushauseberg marches over to us. I try moving my body to the other side of the table hoping he'll ignore the fact we haven't made any progress. No such luck.

"Girls, this is not tea time. Get on with it. Time is ticking away. If your lab is incomplete it's an automatic F." His fingers are tweaking his thick white moustache with glee. Seriously, I hate this guy.

"Not a problem, we're just sorting out a few things," I lie. We barely talked once it became painfully obvious we were forced to be partners. Rebecca has been paired with Krista and it's obvious they're having fun slicing into the formaldehyde-soaked amphibian.

"I hate him," says Megan.

Again she's echoing my thoughts. I smile. "Yeah, totally feel you. So, who's going to do the honors?" My hand holds the scalpel toward her, hoping she'll take it. She looks at me and shakes her head.

Megan swipes her bangs off her forehead and looks at me. "I can't do it but I can't get an F either."

It sounds to me like she's talking more to herself than confessing her hate of this assignment. "Listen, I don't want an F either, but there is no way in hell I can do this."

"How about we do it together?"

"What? I don't think that's a smart move....it's probably not even possible." I say that but I'm thinking it's probably the only way we're going to get through this.

"Listen, we've got to get this over with. Give me that scalpel and place your hand over mine, okay? Then on the count of three we'll make the incision." Megan's sweating and it's pretty obvious, she, like me, is totally out of her element. For once I feel for her.

I hand her the dreaded instrument and nod. "Okay, on the count of three." Placing my hand over hers I notice two things. It's well past manicure time for Megan and her hands feel chapped.

"One. Two. Three," says Megan and immediately I apply pressure to my hand and what do you know, it works.

I see a blue colored vein when we slice open the frog, and when Megan applies more pressure to her hand the mid-section opens. I see a red vein, which means we found an artery. The damn things had been color coded earlier to make it easier for us to see their veins and arteries.

"Kind of cool," says Megan.

I move my hand off hers and pick up a small knife and go around the table so I can help her open the frog all the way. "Yeah, it is. I thought it would be gross. All that red blood and guts stuff which I'm not into, but this isn't that bad."

"Ladies, that's progress. Now don't forget I want you to sketch in detail the heart."

So engrossed at looking at the inside workings of the dead frog, I didn't hear the teacher come to our table.

"Lindsay if you hold this open more, I can get started on the heart," says Megan.

I take over and we switch positions. Megan grabs a piece of paper. I think this is the only class in which pencil and papers are mandatory. Everything else takes place on our laptops. She starts drawing with bold strokes what she's seeing as I hold open the mid-section of the frog. She's good and confident and I realize instantly why Peter asked her to work on the mural. She's an artist.

"That's really good," I say.

She smiles. "Thanks. I used to sketch a lot when I was younger."

"You should keep at it. Do you keep a sketchbook?"

"Again used to," she says. Her eyes become hooded while she purses her lips deep in concentration. "There, I'm done."

"That took you like three minutes. Seriously it's great. And look, we're the first group finished." I can't believe it. After all our stalling at the beginning with Megan's quick art work we're finished. Beaming, I place my hand up.

When the teacher comes over I show him our work. He smiles and says he's pleased we worked together. Since we are done our first lab he offers us the chance to get to work on our second, which he says is more complicated. Megan and I share a look, Basically translated it says, 'bring it on'.

He nods, goes to the back of the lab and opens a locked cabinet. When he brings the large jar over my knees go weak.

"This is a pig fetus. You will need to repeat the exercise you completed but also determine the sex through an internal exam."

Bile rises fast and furious up my windpipe. I cough, hoping to settle my gag reflex down. Not going to happen. Cold sweat breaks out all over my body and my heart's racing that horrible slow thud, meaning I'm about to lose it.

Without saying a word, I dart past the teacher and Megan and storm out of the classroom to the nearest washroom. A few minutes later, with my head still breathing toilet fumes, in walks Megan.

"You okay?" she asks.

I mumble what I'm hoping she'll take as an okay.

Once I'm sure there is nothing left to purge from my stomach, I open the stall door. Megan's wet a piece of paper towel and I use it to wipe my face.

"Thanks," I say.

She doesn't say anything and for a second I wonder if she knows. My face is flushed from my throw-up session but I'm also embarrassed thinking she might know my dirty secret.

"I put everything away from the lab and there's only five

minutes left in class. I told the teacher I was checking up on you and that you mentioned you weren't feeling well earlier."

"Thanks." I'm feeling like a skipping CD, about to get stuck on pause. I look at her and she's watching me.

"Anything you want to tell me?" She asks the question but then turns her attention to washing her hands.

I do the same. "Nope. I'm okay now."

She nods, but I know she's not stupid. Megan's not buying my lie but she's also not asking me to reveal anything specific and I'm grateful for that. If she had asked, I would have had to lie to her because there is no way this secret can get out.

Two more weeks and in more ways than one, all will be purged. That's about the same time as the rec center concert so it looks like that will be my show time.

Chapter 20

Megan

All the way home I'm dealing with the knowing. I should have figured it out earlier. At my old school the symptoms were obvious. Girls leaving to go throw up in the bathroom and voilà what do you know, they are preggers. But Lindsay? No freaking way. She always comes across as hating guys so I'm trying to figure it all out. And who is the lucky daddy?

Barely registering the transfer from one subway to the other, I trek home trying to piece it all together.

"Your Mom and I had a great game of crib," says Mrs. Burrows. I have to side-step to avoid a front on-collision with her.

"That's great. Thanks Mrs. B."

She tisks at me, but deep down I know she likes it when I use her nickname.

"How's things in that fancy school of yours?"

I clutch my laptop closer to my chest and notice the few kids walking close by on the sidewalk. "Great. It's just great."

I open the door to our building for her. "Do us proud," she says. "By the way, I'm on my way to the store. Is there anything you need?"

Shit. If she was visiting with Mom today that means she knows we have absolutely nothing to eat. We finished the milk yesterday and there's only a jar of peanut butter left. "Thanks, Mrs. B but I'm planning to head to the store a bit later." I lie like smooth extra creamy Skippy peanut butter. The expensive kind I had once.

Mrs. B looks at me but doesn't say anything. It's not like she doesn't know our current financial situation, but she's sort of in the same boat. The Canada Pension diet is what she calls it.

"That's good. Tell your mother I'll be wanting a rematch tomorrow." She steps gingerly down the steps. I watch her until she's finished her slow walk down the four steps. Mrs. B has bad arthritis, but she, at least, is able to still walk around the block every day.

I hurry through the dark hall as usual. Opening our door, I dump my stuff inside our apartment as I make my way to the living room. Mom's not there. She must have gotten tired from her cribbage game. When I get near her bedroom I realize she's on the phone with someone. Not wanting to disturb her, I go into my room. The hundred dollars sitting inside my piggy bank, rolled up tight with a blue elastic band, haunts me. That and my stomach. I'm starved.

Sitting on my bed, I examine my options. I could use the money Johnnie left me to buy some food. It's his way of erasing what happened to me, which was all his fault and I'm not feeling the forgiveness mood. Or I could go down two blocks to the food bank. Glancing at my watch, I've got an hour before the food bank closes. Mind made up, I ignore my brother's money, grab my sweater and scribble a note for Mom. As usual I make sure to leave my note in our usual slot—tacked onto the washroom door. Nothing subtle about that, but that's why she insisted on it.

There's a chill in the air and I realize I'm going to need to visit the Salvation Army soon to get a new-to-me winter coat. My next pay cheque from cadets is next week and I'm going to take half of that to start restocking for winter. Boots are always a killer for me. I can usually find a coat that's half decent at a thrift store but when you've got huge feet like me, good luck finding fashionable second hand boots. A flash back to Lindsay's Italian designer boots cuts through me. Quickening my step, I ignore that longing. As well dressed as Lindsay is, she's got stuff going on in her life just like me. There the similarities end.

Making sure my hood is low over my head I walk into the food bank. I hate this place. It has nothing to do with the happy ever-so-helpful volunteers who like to point out my healthy options as they walk me through the aisles, it's the fact I have to come here that kills. Before I get to walk around though, it's registration time.

Megan Avanivitsch. I always spell out my last name. It's not the name I go by at school. There I'm Megan Rockwell. At least I got one good thing from my dead father—his last name I can use at will. Since Mom didn't change her last name when she got married I had used her name when I started school in my neighborhood.

Use it once and it's tagged on you for life. There's nothing complicated with Rockwell but there is always spelling and then questions when people hear my real last name. Is that Russian or Croatian? Try Polish. Answering that always enlists a slew of other questions I never want to answer.

"Good to see you again Megan," says Ms. Lynn. She's got to be the happiest person walking this planet. She's always smiling and has a kind word for everyone, including her normal grumpy clients, like Mr. Fischer who is waiting not-so-patiently in line behind me.

"Get on with it. We don't have all night for this," says Mr. Fischer, whose breath reeks of cigarettes. He's wearing his usual outfit. A gray mechanic overall that has more grease on it than anything else. Mr. Fischer is about eighty and shouldn't have to work any longer but he does. His story—a sick wife. Since I discovered that I don't get so angry when Mr. Fischer starts to curse under his breath.

"Oh, Mr. Fischer, don't you worry your soul. We won't let you leave empty handed."

He calls her a few choice words, making me cringe. I'm glad Ms. Lynn didn't hear him but knowing her, even if she did, she wouldn't let that faze her.

"Now, Megan what do you and your mother need today?" Ms. Lynn takes out a white piece of paper so she can diligently write down everything I take. When I asked her once why she did that she got flustered and in a hushed voice said she had to account for all the food, because her workers have been known to accidentally take things and with government funding so tight for food banks she had to account for the need within the community. Our neighborhood screams need everywhere. It's graffiti scrawled on most of the buildings but the politicians have yet to learn how to read *our* language.

My eyes dart around the place. Over a decade ago, it used to be a Swiss Chalet. When things went bust in my neighborhood the city bought the building for next to nothing and ever since, it's been a food bank. When I first started coming here before Mom found it too difficult to get here by wheelchair, I swear to god you could smell roasting chicken from when it used to be a restaurant. It always made me hungry. That smell has been replaced with the overpowering odor of onions, and the not-so-subtle aroma of rotting produce.

I pick up the usual. Five cans of no-name soup, two chicken noodle, two mushroom and one celery. That's the entire selection of soup. I place my stuff in the small steel basket I'm holding in my hand. I move to the bread section and take three loaves.

"Sorry we're all out of eggs," says Ms. Lynn. "But you come back tomorrow and I'll put two dozen aside for you and your mother."

I wish I could but tomorrow is a school day and the food bank doesn't open until ten in the morning. Like she sees my dilemma, Ms. Lynn gives a quiet chuckle.

"Oh, silly me. You've got school tomorrow morning. Don't you worry. I'll put them aside and you can pop down tomorrow night. Okay?"

I nod, too overcome to speak for a moment. She doesn't say anything else, just leads me to the meat section. Today the special is liver and chicken giblets. Wow, surprises never end. I take the smallest selections I can get away with, knowing Ms. Lynn is all in favor of animal organs. She once gave me a lecture on their properties when she heard me groan. I wanted to tell her my groan had nothing to do with the meats and all to do with selection. I bypass the fish section and thank god my mom lied to Ms. Lynn saying I had an allergy. The first time we took fish from here we both got sick as dogs. After that Mom said no more fish. Her reasoning is that a little white lie saves face. I didn't say anything. At the time I was eight and I was only too happy to avoid having to eat the smelly stuff.

Ms. Lynn plops a cauliflower in my basket. I eye it but don't point out it's half rotten.

Ms. Lynn catches my look.

"Just cut that half off. It's still good."

Funny how she can say that but avoid looking me in the eye.

Mentally I steel myself to get it together. I tuck a stray hair behind my ear and give a half-hearted smile and nod, but I start to look at my sneakers when she also puts a bag of mushy carrots in my basket along with a bag of apples. The apples don't look so bad so that's a plus.

"Got any peanut butter?" I ask, watching as more and more

people come through the door.

"Not out front, but let me check in the back."

She darts off before I can tell her to forget it. I'm left dealing with that nervous feeling I always get when I come to the food bank. A lot of my *had been* friends from my old school come here so I try to time my grocery shopping around when they are least likely to drop in. After school is a good time, because the girls from my old school always hang around the rink so they can watch the boys. I never did that because I always felt I had to get home to Mom. They started to shun me when they heard the news I was changing schools, anyway. Things went from bad to ugly quickly.

I'm wishing I hadn't asked about peanut butter when Carmelita walks in. She used to be my BFF. Not anymore. She takes one glance at me and then turns her head. Chewing a wad of purple bubble gum she marches to the front. Loud as can be she cites off her name, which she too spells out because like me she's got Polish blood and just like me it's her and her mom. Those two things used to unite us. Not anymore. I notice she's wearing brand new jeans and her long black hair is swept up in a fashionable ponytail. She looks the same but different.

She saunters toward me and I can't move.

"So how's that Prep school?" asks Carmelita, stunning the hell out of me.

The only other time we got close to each other in the summer she was with our usual gang of girlfriends and she pointedly told me I was a fucking whore who thought I was better than the rest of them. I kept my mouth shut like crazy glue and only cried when I got home. They don't understand me. When the army cadet recruitment team came to our school in grade seven I tried to get the girls, and especially Carmelita, to come with me. She came to one class but that was it. She wasn't wasting her time with a bunch of stupid people marching around for show. I knew then and there things were never going to be the same. I viewed school as a way out of my neighborhood and cadets was a helping ladder to accomplish all that.

"Okay." I move my basket to my other arm.

She nods, like she gets that. I'm a little unsure what to say or ask.

"How are things with you?" I ask, pleased when Ms. Lynn

comes back in carrying two jars of peanut butter.

"Same. Oh thanks, Ms. Lynn." Carmelita flashes a smile up at her but I see the sadness in her eyes.

Carmelita is an even five feet. She's tiny all the way around. As sweet as she usually is she can get downright mean when she needs to and in my neighborhood that's okay. We used to laugh together because her potty mouth always got her in trouble in school but that same mouth often saved our hides on the streets.

"I saw you come in Carmelita. It's so good to see you two girls and I know I'm not supposed to say that because I'm always hoping you won't have need to come here but seeing you both brightens my day."

I've known Carmelita since I turned five. We shared a lot of stuff together but over the course of the last year we stopped seeing each other. I kept what happened to me quiet but I get the distinct impression she has her own share of secrets. At one time we took a blood oath promising to always share. Guess adolescence changed all that. Or the fact telling some secrets out loud really is just too painful to bear.

"You are as sweet as ever," says Carmelita to Ms. Lynn, earning major brownie points from her.

Ms. Lynn's niceness is like a perfume that permeates inside you without you even knowing it. Ms. Lynn carefully drops a jar of no-name extra crunchy peanut butter in my basket, letting it rest on top of my meats. It's the type I hate, but beggars can't be choosers. Since there's nothing yet in Carmelita's basket she places the other jar, an extra smooth type I would love to get my hands on, inside hers. I can't help but watch it roll around when Carmelita moves the large basket to her other hand.

I'm finished and there's no point in sticking around. I make my way to the front so I can sign off on the registration index card that notes the date, time and quantity of the stuff I needed. I've always hated this part.

Once I'm at the door, I hear Carmelita call my name.

"Wait a sec, Megan."

I wait, but I'm dreading it. She ushers me out of the door and once we're on the sidewalk which I notice is filled with gobs of gum, she drops the two almost see-through plastic bags she's gotten. I'm not sure what she's doing until she digs out the peanut butter.

“Let’s switch, okay?” she asks.

I smile. “Yeah, I’d love that.”

“I know. You always hated those bits of peanuts,” she says, laughing.

I laugh along with her and feel a sense of relief.

This day is full of surprises.

Chapter 21

Lindsay

Should have known Rebecca wasn't going to give up on her idea of scoring a romantic getaway with Blair and the gang. Her original weekend fell through because Blair had a hockey tournament. Oh what a shame, not! And silly me with it being Thursday, and so close to the end of the week, I had thought for sure she wouldn't have time to put together a new plan. Yet the text message to me clearly outlines *said* plan.

Not only am I forced into lying if Rebecca's Mom calls my cell but I'm forced to lie to my mother. Lying is no problem, usually, but if my mother's got her lying-radar on, when she's not focused one hundred percent on something to do with work, then it's a big problem. Funny how she can sniff out a lie, but doesn't want to know the ugly truth taking place in her own house.

"Mother, Rebecca and I are all heading to Krista's for a sleepover." I make sure not to ask permission. Asking always sets off questions. I also make sure I'm at the door, fully loaded with my getaway sleepover backpack, and time my little bomb when her Blackberry rings.

"Okay, have fun. You're back on Sunday."

It's not a question, either. Mumbling, "Yeah," I grab my stuff and haul it out before she thinks to ask me a dozen motherly questions. The one question I wish she'd ask she doesn't.

A block away from the house, I re-read Rebecca's instructions. I'm to meet up with her and Krista at the school and then we're taking the subway to the east end to some dive of a hotel that Rebecca booked using her platinum credit card. A month ago she made a point of telling us her card wasn't tied to her parents and they simply dropped three thousand dollars every month into her savings account. Krista moaned with longing. I didn't say anything. I'm not hurting for money and if my mother knew how

Rebecca's parents work, I'm sure she would find a way to make sure I'm set up like her. But, I don't want it. Mother forks over enough hundred dollar bills my way to make me feel sleazy. Case in point the one she practically threw at me when I opened the door to leave. Still cradling her phone on her shoulder, she had flipped open a binder tucked under her arm and yet she still managed to whip out her wallet to take out money for me. Some kids would think that was love. I know better.

"Oh my god, I thought you weren't coming." Krista is all but bouncing on the spot. Rebecca laughs at her, but then loops me into a hug. I notice again they've coordinated their outfits. Tight jeans, sweaters and black high heeled boots.

"Next stop the drugstore." Rebecca says drugstore real slow, like it's a place none of us frequent. It dawns on me then what she's looking to buy. Condoms.

"I'm not going to a drugstore, Rebecca." I let her take my arm and the three of us make our way to the subway tunnel.

Rebecca's flicking her long hair out of her face when she says, "Good point. We shouldn't do a drugstore here in case someone we know walks in."

That's not what I meant. Instead, I don't say anything and let them drag me along. I didn't want to come but going against Rebecca is something I'm not strong enough to face. We're a giggling mess by the time we board the subway. For me it's totally fake, as usual. Not the case for Krista and Rebecca. The beginnings of a migraine start to pound behind my temples but I'm hoping it's because of the rumbling of the subway coming our way.

Krista elbows me.

"Stop that," I say.

She leans closer. "Don't look but that guy is totally checking you out. And he's hot."

"Yeah, he is," says Rebecca, with a giggle.

I don't turn around and when I don't I get another poke from Krista.

We're forced like rats to move through the maze of people to get onto the subway. "What's up with you?" Krista whispers loud enough for me to hear.

I give her a droll look I've mastered. "You told me not to look so I didn't."

"I didn't really mean it," she says.

"Yeah, but how was I to know that? Plus I'm not interested in some guy."

Rebecca leans on me and giggles again and I'm starting to wonder if she's high. "Yeah, that's right. Linds is only interested in one man."

I don't bother responding. "How long before we're there?" I'm starting to feel nauseous again and wish I had thought to bring along a power bar. Instead I reach into my purse and search for some gum. I've taken to chewing spearmint gum because it usually helps. Panic sets in when I realize I'm all out. I chewed my last one in chemistry class this afternoon. "Anyone got any gum?" My mouth feels dry and I'm praying one of them has something. "Or anything." I force myself to relax.

Krista looks at me like I'm nuts. She already lectured me on how uncool chewing gum is. I didn't say anything then and I'm not about to speak up now.

Rebecca hands me a mint without even looking at me. She's too busy checking out the people checking her out. That's the thing with Rebecca. She's tall, classically beautiful with that flawless complexion you get from regular maintenance at a spa and she's draped in designer duds and actress-modeled jewelry. We're on a subway and heading to the east end of town and they are most certainly not dressed to fit in.

The subway makes a hard stop, forcing me to clutch at the hand rail in front of me. When we stop I look out.

There on the platform, staring at me like she's seeing a freaking ghost is Megan. I blink. What the hell is she wearing? It looks like a green army uniform. I'm about to point her out to Krista and Rebecca but something holds me back. She darts behind a few people trying to get on the subway and then before I know it she's gone. For a second I wonder if I imagined it but then that look of absolute horror on her face flashes through my mind and I know there is no way it wasn't Megan.

"Why are you so quiet?" asks Rebecca. She's forced us into seats reserved for seniors. Awkward. I glance at an old lady standing, her grip tight on the hand rail. I make a move to get up, but Rebecca places her hand on my leg.

"We're good. Don't worry about it."

It? It's not an it. It's an elderly lady. Standing, I look down at Rebecca and Krista, and realize something—I don't like them. It's not a revelation that stuns me but it is an awakening of sorts.

"These seats are reserved for the elderly." I hate the fact I have to whisper my point to them.

"So what?" says Krista, fishing around in her designer purse for something. When she pulls out pink lipstick I roll my eyes. I'm also hoping the subway lurches fast and she's left with streaks across her face.

"So, get up." I follow through, forcing them to move but not without dramatic sighs of annoyance from both of them.

"Those seats are free," I say to the old lady.

"That's very kind of you. Thanks so much."

She smiles at me and for the first time that day I feel good.

Once we're finally at our stop all that good feeling dissipates like a hot Mexican downpour. Soaked to the bone one minute but then dry as the desert the next. There standing on the platform are the guys—Blair, Derek, Jeff and just my luck, Connor. We step off the subway and both Krista and Rebecca run into the arms of their guys. Slowly I walk forward, with dread a heavy weight pulling down my new red Italian leather boots. The only one watching me with a look that conveys how he feels is Jeff. That could be because for once there isn't a game in his hands and it makes him look vulnerable and awkward. Since that's how I'm feeling, I'm almost wishing I had thrown up. Puking my guts out would definitely get me kicked out of this weekend but it wouldn't be worth the questions and lies I'd be forced to regurgitate.

Rebecca, the mascot for the group, says, "This is going to be so cool."

I step in behind the group, mumbling, "Yeah." Rebecca gives me a look that says get with the happy program, Linds.

"Lame is more like it," says Jeff, shocking me. Honestly, it's the first time I've heard him speak. When I was introduced to him in September he flicked his brown eyes up at me and then tuned back into his game. I had tried to ask him what he was playing but after getting no response I stopped.

"Like I said earlier to the guys, Rebecca, I can't stay the entire night." Connor's got a blush the hue of a red corvette on his brown cheeks. He darts a look at me but he's talking to Rebecca who is linked arm-in-arm with Blair.

"That's okay, right?" asks Rebecca, turning to wink at me. "We can have lots of fun before midnight."

I don't say anything. This time I also don't nod. Connor looks at me and I glare back at him. I made it plain like yogurt we were friends. Nothing more. I let Rebecca and Blair and Krista and Derek walk ahead. Jeff follows next to Blair and they're chatting away at something, which makes Rebecca laugh. For a minute I wonder if they're talking about me. Connor drops behind and what do you know, we're walking side by side.

"Sorry about that. Rebecca seems to have plans for us. I tried to tell her we're just friends but she's not into that. Good thing I'm leaving at midnight," says Connor. He stuffs a hand into his front pant pocket and his head hangs low, like he's ashamed of something. Probably ashamed of me.

I pick up my pace and say, "Yeah, I tried to tell her too. But like I said before it's not going to happen."

He laughs a soft chuckle a normal girl would like. Jeff's head swivels around and he gives us a hard look. Weird.

"I get that. Don't worry. It's cool by me. We'll just sit outside the room and chat okay?"

I stop and look at him. He is totally cool with it. I smile. "Thanks. That would be cool."

It's then I notice he's brought a large backpack. "What's with the backpack if you're not spending the night?"

Connor grins. "Well, after I heard you've never tried Indian food I thought to change all that tonight. With my luck though it will be cold and the hotel room won't have a microwave. It's not gourmet but you can't say you've lived until you try Indian food."

I laugh, startling myself. "Thanks. I'd love to try it, but you shouldn't have."

"Actually, I had to. When I told my mom what you said I had to practically hold her down. She threatened to come over to your house with a meal and I'm not kidding."

"Do you tell your Mom everything?"

A contemplative look passes across his face. "Yeah, I do. She's the world for me."

"You're really lucky." *In more ways than one.*

"I know. Trust me though, when I told her I was meeting up

with the gang tonight she insisted I bring food along for you to try. I'm warning you now, she'll probably ask you what you thought of it the next time she sees you. And I'm going to beg a big favor here, but can you please tell her you liked it?"

"Come on you two love birds, move it," hollers Rebecca. Her Colgate smile would make an ad agency happy. Her match-making innuendoes make me sick.

I put my hand on Connor's arm. "Thanks. No matter what I will tell your mother I loved it." In truth, I'll probably puke my guts out but I can't tell him that.

"Thanks. That makes me feel better."

We don't say anything else as we catch up to the group. Jeff keeps darting odd looks my way and I have no idea why.

Once we clear the subway tunnel we head down the street. Rebecca gets real close to Blair, who's got his macho stride on. The east end of town is not pretty. The conversation stops once the reality of where we are settles in. We walk in a tight group down the sidewalk, which is littered with broken beer bottles, empty soda cans and garbage. We pass a large block filled with run down apartments making you think no one can live in them but when we notice a few lights on you realize people do. Scary. There are stores with steel cages as their front décor and the area might as well be renamed graffiti lane because of the amount of spray paint scrawled over the bricks.

By the time we come to the motel, I'm thinking Rebecca's changed her mind. I know I am. The place creeps me out. A neon motel sign spells out TEL, because the MO were smashed a long time ago and no one bothered to fix them. It's a taunting flickering orange that screams 'Tell someone you are here and then run'. Straight out of a horror flick, the motel is one long block of one-storey cement units. At one time the front door had been painted a bright apple color red, but now the mostly peeled entrance way showcases neglect and an 'I don't care and won't ask' vibe.

"You all stay here. The reservation is in Blair's and mine's name as Mr. and Mrs. Johnson."

"Johnson?" asks Jeff, clearly finding that name amusing.

"It was better than Smith," says Blair, laughing.

The rest of us keep silent. A vision of bed bugs running all over me causes me to cringe.

Like she read my mind, Krista pipes up. "I am sooo not taking my clothes off in that place."

"I'm not asking you to take all of them off," says Derek, grabbing Krista for a quick hug. I think his comment is gross but she doesn't.

"There's a picnic table by the side over there, once they get settled we'll eat our food over there," says Connor.

I nod at him.

A few minutes later out walk Rebecca and Blair and what do you know, Rebecca's waving a unit key. Just our luck the no-question policy was alive and kicking tonight.

"Money talks, Linds," says Rebecca. She looks like she's won the lotto. "We're in number 69, isn't that funny?" Only the couples giggle. Jeff groans like he's been stabbed and Connor and I don't say anything.

I'm praying a big cockroach party will greet us when we open the door. Rebecca gives Blair the key so he can open the rickety door. We all file through and take stock of the unit. One double-bed with a green and pink bedspread with stains near the edges, a white microwave which makes Connor happy, a flickering bathroom light and an old-fashioned TV that takes up most of the small top of the bureau. Honestly, the TV looks like someone picked it up from a dumpster. When a cockroach crawls out from under the bed, Rebecca marches over to it without a word and uses her boot to smash it to smithereens. Krista squeals but Derek's arms are holding her tight.

Guess getting sex for them means they won't let a bug get in their way. I resist the urge to point out bed bugs bite and can leave a nasty red rash on your body. Since I'm not taking one thing off and don't plan on staying any longer than five minutes in said room, I'm hoping the bed bugs go to town on them. After all, they deserve what they get.

I, on the other hand, don't deserve what I've gotten. Getting knocked up by your step-father is not only illegal, but the shame I feel makes me feel like that smashed cockroach. Dead.

Chapter 22

Megan

What are the freaking odds I'd be standing on the subway platform waiting for my ride in my army uniform only to see Lindsay and her friends staring at me? Guess one hundred percent. Panicking probably didn't do me any favors and I'm sure they're laughing their asses off. What the hell were they doing on the subway? I know Lindsay hates them and I'm fairly certain both Krista and Rebecca's rich, snobby parents would freak if they found out their precious daughters were low-balling it to the subway for the east end of town.

"Everything all right?" Master Windemere's voice drills into me.

"Fine, Sir." My voice is totally in control. No way do I want the Master's fatherly concern nailing me. He's been helpful for me but sometimes, like now, I need time to digest what happened.

"Dismissed," he says.

Automatically, my legs move while my feet march. Once we're off parade the new recruits go over to chat with their beaming friends and parents. Tonight was an orientation night and it always kills me. All those parents looking on with pride makes me long for something I can't have. Mom's never made it to one orientation night. Then again I've never told her about them so feeling hurt is self-induced.

After I ditch my army uniform I basically run home. It's Friday night and as usual I'll be doing nothing. For once I don't mind. I open the apartment door, but Mom doesn't answer me with her usual. "Hi, how was it?" Instead, I find my neighbor sitting on our sofa.

"Mrs. B, everything all right?" I ask it but know the answer already. Mom's had another episode. But there's something in

Mrs. Burrows eyes warning me it's not good.

Mrs. B gets up and shuffles toward me. She clutches the small table next to the sofa and she's shaking. I urge her to sit and then she tells me everything that happened. By the end of her halting conversation I'm the one shaking. Mom's back in the hospital but this time she probably won't be coming home any time soon.

I get Mrs. B settled quickly back into her apartment and then gather my stuff. I hustle it to the hospital. Briefly I think about calling Johnnie. I know I should but something stops me.

Recycled air, over-used Javex enhanced floor polish and that underlying reek of sickness greets me when I go to the hospital's front desk to ask what room my mom's in. The answer startles me. Surgery. That I didn't expect.

Sitting down in the waiting room I eye the black public phone in the lobby. Finally I gather my courage and drop a quarter into the phone. No surprise when Johnnie doesn't answer. I leave a succinct message and then return to the waiting room to watch the clock.

Three hours later in walks Johnnie, wearing designer jeans and a white and blue striped shirt. He got a haircut and he looks more together. He sits across from me, nods his head but doesn't say anything, which infuriates me. Not even a how's Mom?

"I talked to the nurse at the front desk and she said Mom will be out of surgery in about another hour but we'll have a wait until we get to see her."

Oh, he talked to someone. Now I understand why he didn't hit the list of questions.

He leans forward bracing his arms on his knees. I can't help but notice he's wearing black Italian loafers. Just when did Johnnie start to dress like this? He catches my look but says nothing. "Did she talk to you about it?"

He's referring to Mom's brain tumor. The tumor I had no idea she had. This time it's me shaking my head.

He leans back and says, "Yeah, that's just like her to not tell us. She didn't want to worry us."

Once again I nod. I notice only ten minutes have clocked by and we're the only ones left sitting in the waiting room. Was it only four hours ago I was thinking this Friday night would be like all the same—boring? That nervous, fearful feeling skating through me is not what I want.

"Have you had anything to eat?" Johnnie looks at me and then gets up without a word.

I thought of lying but he'd know. About twenty minutes later he returns with two pre-packaged vendor sandwiches, a cup of coffee, a bag of chips and two chocolate bars. I already know which bar is his—Oh Henry. When we were younger the food bank was a treasure trove of Oh Henry bars after Halloween thanks to the generous donation of parents not wanting to let their kids take peanuts to school. That first time when Johnnie came back loaded with Oh Henry bars I called him Oh Johnnie, especially since he ate so many he ended up with a stomachache. Mom said it served him right. I just kept saying Oh Johnnie, until he threw a pillow at me. Closing my eyes I realize that was six years ago. Now everything has changed between us.

Chowing down on the vendor sandwich I don't even notice what's inside it. Going on automatic I also eat the chips, sip my coffee and slowly eat my bar. I sniffle, feeling sad but pleased Johnnie remembered Aero bars are my favorite.

"It's going to be okay, Megan," says Johnnie.

"How come you never said sorry to me when it happened?"

Johnnie leans back into the hard plastic chair. There are four dark blue chairs connected together in one row. I wonder if they were designed that way so people like me who have to wait hours can flake out on them.

He runs his hands through his hair. "I was too ashamed at myself for not believing you. I couldn't believe Cody would do that to you and honestly, I didn't want to believe it." He leans back and looks at the clock on the wall. Hope he finds inspiration from it because I certainly don't. "I didn't know what to think but when I confronted him…"

There's a long pause. Finally Johnnie leans forward and forces me to look at him. "I took care of Cody for you, Megan. He won't forget what he did to you anytime soon. And trust me, he won't bother you again."

That's not what I wanted to hear but it doesn't surprise me. In our neighborhood, the rules of the street that allow him to think an eye for an eye aren't right but it's our form of justice. I don't want to know what he did to his friend. It will only make me feel worse.

"I went to the clinic up the street and got a morning after pill." My voice is flat, dead of emotion.

"Fuck." He wipes his hands on his new jeans. "Jesus Megan, I'm sorry. I know nothing I can do will fix what he did, but honestly I was so high I didn't know what he was doing."

I whisper the words he needs to hear. "I know. I forgive you."

"Jesus Megan, how can you?"

That's the question now rattling around in my brain. He brought the evil into our apartment and his friend took something precious from me. As much as I want to blame my brother I can't. No matter what, Johnnie is my brother and he's someone I once loved something fierce. "You didn't mean to."

"I'm in treatment for my addiction." He turns his head to look toward the front desk and then looks at me. I return the look.

"I'm also working. A real job."

"Really?"

"Yeah." He laughs and I notice how at twenty-one, he looks a lot older. That's the thing with my neighborhood, poverty is the best face cream on the market if you want to look older than your years.

"You will never guess who I'm working for."

Taking another sip of my quick-cooling coffee, I urge him on with a nod. As my brother, he knows my gestures and damn if I don't like that. There's no pretending and often no need for words.

"Your Commanding Officer's brother."

"What?" I sit up, totally paying attention now.

"Yeah, funny world isn't it?" He's relaxing a bit now that there's been a shift in the conversation, but also because we're mending what we once had.

We're both trying hard to ignore the bomb of discovery that Mom has a brain tumor but you can feel its heavy silence ticking silently away between us.

My eyes dart to the door when a cold draft sails in. In walks a woman with an older lady, who you know is her mom. She's urging her mom to the check in area but the old lady isn't budging. I'm glad when the nurses rush forward to help.

I refocus my attention back to Johnnie. "So, tell me exactly what you're doing."

He starts talking and by the end I'm smiling. It is funny how life works out. Turns out Master Windemere's brother runs a high-end furniture making store. One day he spotted Johnnie sitting on a step whittling, as usual, with his knife and a piece of wood. They struck up a conversation but Johnnie didn't follow up until a few weeks ago. Until after he saved me, until after we had our big blow up. I wonder about that but don't say anything until he's done telling me his story.

The short of it is Mr. David Windemere offered him a job with the understanding he has to attend Community College in the day to work on getting his journeyman carpentry papers. He gets paid a regular wage plus he gets seventy percent profit on any of his own works he sells in the shop. Turns out his fingers know how to work with wood, and it's paying off. This week alone he sold four of his wooden figurines for a total of over four hundred dollars.

I feel real proud of him and Mom would be too.

We both sit up when we spot a doctor walking toward us still in his blue scrubs. I get a flash of all those doctor shows on TV and hope we're the lucky couple. As the doctor gets closer my hands start to sweat. Johnnie's are too because he keeps wiping them on his jeans. I place my hand on his and squeeze. He looks at me and says nothing, but nods.

After a few polite words the doctor sits down next to Johnnie. I hear him talking. He's saying a lot of big words I totally get, but know Johnnie doesn't. Ignorance is bliss I think as the doctor goes on and on.

Johnnie leans in closer to the doctor. "Basically you're saying my mom's a vegetable?"

Ah, the brutal truth summed up in one word. The doctor clears his throat, starts to mumble something but then changes his mind.

"We're just not sure. The tumor was a lot bigger than we thought and as I told your mom when she came in last time it's cancerous. We did manage to remove most of it, but we're not sure how far it's spread. Brain surgery is delicate."

"No shit," says Johnnie, leaning back into the chair, like he's trying to catch his breath.

I totally get that because I'm finding it hard to breathe.

"Normally for someone with her condition we wouldn't undertake such a risky procedure." I notice the doctor's wringing his hands.

"Thanks for doing it." I force the doctor to look at me for the first time. I'm usually in Johnnie's shadow when he's around because he's older and a lot bigger than me. I lean forward so I can see the doctor's pale blue eyes better. He looks tired, just how I feel. He's only human.

"When can we see her?" Silently, I'm praying he's somehow pulled off a miracle with Mom.

"She'll have to remain in intensive care for a few days but we'll keep you informed of her progress. Always the first twenty-four hours are critical. A lot can happen. Swelling of the brain isn't uncommon and with her pre-existing condition…"

The doctor goes on and on and by the time he's done listing all the types of complications and potentially what we might expect for an outcome both Johnnie and I are speechless. Before he leaves, Johnnie gives the doctor his cell number. He urges us to go home and rest with the promise they'll call us the minute we're allowed in to see our mom.

We both nod, mumbling thanks again, like that's all we can say.

Thanks for nothing, is what I'm thinking.

Chapter 23

Lindsay

"This is great." I'm eating the food Connor brought and honestly I love it. It tastes like nothing I have ever tried before. It's hot, thanks to the oh-my-god-working microwave and it's got a texture of spices that my palate strangely likes. My stomach isn't rolling around in waves like it's getting ready to revolt all on its own. That's how it felt when I ate the spaghetti we had for supper last night. My quick bolt to the washroom only pissed off Mother. She likes to pretend to Greg she's taught me manners. Truthfully she hasn't, but I force myself to play her game because having her harp at me isn't worth it.

When I was younger I didn't mind. But when I was younger my mother was normal. Not a multi-million dollar lady determined to make a difference in the corporate world she calls home. I'm not sure exactly when she shifted from my mother to a business-lady with one goal in mind but I do remember my first nanny. She wasn't a trained nanny or anything like that, and she was sort of okay, if you liked to eat tomato soup and bologna every other day. She lasted six months and by the end of it, the smell of bologna made my gag reflex act up.

I bite another pastry he called a Samosa. Spicy vegetables make me groan.

"I'm glad you like it," says Connor. "So, how long do you plan on staying outside?"

"The entire night," I mumble, not wanting to give up eating. Connor laughs.

"Yeah, I get that, but you're going to get cold. Why don't you just go home?"

Ah, the crux of the matter. "Can't. I promised Rebecca I'd stay." Plus she'd ditch me if I left. I keep that thought to myself.

"Seriously, you're planning on spending the night outside?"

"Yup."

Without a word Connor gets up from the picnic table. "Where are you going?" I call out, anxious because if he's trying to be my white knight tonight it's not going to work. I stuff the food boxes back in the plastic bag he brought and follow after him. "Don't."

"This is ridiculous. It's not right."

"Yeah, I know but having Rebecca totally pissed at me won't make things better."

"Well, you can't stay outside all night."

Before I can tell him to knock on the door to the dingy motel room he opens it. The two couples are so busy going at it they barely register the cold blast of air that sails into the room with us. I'm hoping they'll catch a cold.

"Oh, Linds and Connor are joining us," says Rebecca. Her shirt and bright red bra are on the floor and I'm shocked she's marshaled a bit of modesty by pulling up the stained bedspread almost to her neck. I'm hoping she's got her pants on but wouldn't be surprised if they are on the other side of the bed next to Krista and Derek, who are totally still making out.

"Actually, we're not joining you. Lindsay and I are heading home," says Connor. He's got one foot in the door but his hand is still on the door knob. I can tell by his strained facial muscles he's not impressed with the scene. Maybe his mom really did teach him manners.

"Linds, what's he talking about? You can't go home."

I'm about to speak up but Connor's totally cloaked in his shining-knight armor. "She's coming with me or you can all come with us. This place is totally gross."

It is but obviously what they are doing outweighs the filth of this place. Both Rebecca and Blair laugh, causing Derek to lift his head off of Krista's neck. She's got a huge red mark on the side of her neck and I'm wondering how she's going to explain that to her parents. Then it dawns on me Jeff isn't here. I don't remember him leaving. There's a light on in the bathroom. He wouldn't be in there, would he?

Before I stop myself, I walk over to it and gently knock on it. "Jeff, you in there?"

He opens the door. I'm wondering what he was doing but know instantly he was gaming. Except when I look down at the device in his hand I notice it's turned off.

"You two have fun out there?" asks Jeff, looking at me with that weird look.

Moving out of his way he cuts past me toward the open door.

"Ah, sort of, what gives with you?" I ask, starting to really hate his attitude. I might not talk to him but I'm not overly rude either.

Jeff doesn't answer me. Instead he announces, "I'm leaving with Connor and Lindsay. See you later Blair." Jeff's announcement deflates the last bubble of happiness in the room.

"Wait a sec, stay man." Blair's pushing Rebecca to the side so he can crawl over her. I'm praying he's got his pants still on. And what do you know for once the guy upstairs is smiling down at me. Not caring people are watching him, Blair rearranges his privates, which makes Jeff look down at the brown crusty shag carpet. Blair drapes an arm chum-like around Jeff, drawing him in close so he can whisper something private in his ear. Jeff shrugs his shoulders and steps out of Blair's hold. Totally weird.

Without a word Jeff grabs his jacket he had draped over the TV. Blair tries to talk to him again, but he's out the door so fast we're all wondering what's up with him. Wanting to leave, I follow. In another minute I hear Connor's steps join us. We silently make our way from the motel to the subway stop. It's probably close to midnight and I'm wondering if Connor's going to get in trouble for staying out past his curfew.

"That was weird," says Connor when he's closer to me.

No weirder than how Jeff's acting, I think. Up ahead Jeff's silhouette is outlined thanks to some of the working street lights. He's not waiting for us and I'm okay with that. I wonder if Rebecca and Krista have resumed their make-out sessions or if they're checking out. Whatever happens I know I'll be getting a call from Rebecca soon that won't go well for me. *Whatever*. Not like she's my only worry at the moment.

"Yeah, Jeff's always been different and intense, but he's sort of okay." I have no idea why I feel the need to defend Jeff. Honestly, I barely know him. Then again he certainly doesn't know me. And maybe that's why I feel like someone should stick up for him.

At the subway stop, Jeff surprises us by waiting at the top of the long stairs that lead to the underground tunnel. Without a word, we walk down the filthy steps and what do you know, that welcoming smell of urine and body odor gags me as we get lower and closer to the platform. Jeff probably wants the company because three people together are better than going solo in this neighborhood. Once we're on the platform I notice the two homeless people huddled in the far corner where the lights are out. They've got bags surrounding them.

"Connor, do you have any more food?" I ask.

Connor looks at me and smiles. "Sure do. Great idea." Quickly he takes out the plastic containers still loaded with food. "You coming?" He's looking at Jeff, not me.

"You guys are nuts," says Jeff, but his feet follow after us.

When we get closer I notice both are old ladies. Well, I think they're old but it's hard to tell with the layers of filth covering them. "Would you like some Indian food? It's not too spicy and while it's not that hot any longer, it's really good."

The younger lady smiles at us, and drops ten years with that one gesture. I estimate she's mid-thirties and while I'm wondering how she found herself in this predicament that's not why we are here.

She stands, and I bet she's wearing four layers of clothing. I would too if I had to live on the street. They are huddled near an in-take valve. Smart. The heat from the vent must be a welcome relief.

"Thank you so much." She accepts the containers from Connor with ease and grace, causing me to feel shame. I'm wishing I had something more to give her. Connor slips off his black down jacket. The lady shakes her head.

"Come on, it will help." He flashes that charming smile of his and she accepts his gift. A blush of thanks softens her grimy looks. She's got a wool cap on over her dirt-brown hair that could use a good shampoo and cut.

When Jeff follows suit, slipping of his long wool men's coat with ease I'm stunned. He slips out a business card and hands it to the lady.

"I couldn't," says the lady, who's looking at Jeff like he's a miracle worker.

I have no idea what she's talking about and neither does Connor. We're both casting glances at Jeff, but he's ignoring us.

Jeff steps forward more into the lady's space. "Tell her Jeff sent you. She'll help you get things set up and not only that but she'll treat you both right." His speech slips from his formal one-wordiness to almost street slang.

The loud rumbling of the subway is our departure cue. Once again I'm reminded of Megan's words about how you feel the subway long before you see it. She's right and that simple observation sums her up. Megan isn't like Rebecca or Krista. I'm not sure who she's like, but while I'm standing there in the middle of the night on the platform I know she's the person I want to talk to first thing in the morning. I'm not going to ask her about the uniform. I've got a feeling that wouldn't go so well. Like me, Megan's layers cover up more than her body.

"Thank you. Thank you so much," says the lady, bobbing her head at us.

"What's your names?"

Jesus I can't believe I never thought to ask. I'm further surprised Jeff did.

"Betty and this is my sister, Sally."

Sally just nods but doesn't say anything.

"How long you been on the streets Betty?"

"Just a few months…hard times and all…and Sally doesn't like to be away from me so I can't leave her alone…" she pulls her cap low like she knows how bad she looks.

A few months? Holy shit, I can't believe that. She looks like she's been on the street for years.

"Well Sally, you take Betty with you and I'm going to check up to make sure you showed up, okay?"

When did Jeff start to sound like Dr. Phil? I look at him, thinking I don't know anyone anymore.

The subway groans to a stop. We all nod at the ladies and then make our way through the automatic sliding doors, minus food and two jackets.

"Okay Jeff, what gives?" I force him to look at me once we claim the row of hard plastic seats.

"My aunt runs a shelter on 6th and Tisle Street. I help out after school on Tuesdays and Thursdays."

My heart's beating fast and it's got nothing to do with what just happened and a lot to do with his disclosure. Tisle Street is where the abortion clinic is. In fact it's located on the corner of 6th, not that most people would know that. It looks like one of Toronto's average non-descript brown-brick buildings except it's far from ordinary. My eyes dart to his. Last week after school on Thursday I walked through the doors of the clinic for a consultation.

Jeff stares back at me. He doesn't need to say anything else. I get it. He knows.

I'm glad when Connor starts to ask him questions about the shelter. When Connor says he'd like to help out, this time it's Jeff who is surprised.

"You sure about that? It's not the best part of the city to be in."

"You go, so I'm sure it will be fine. Plus, I like to help people. Must be in my blood," says Connor, chuckling a little, trying hard to diffuse the awkward situation. I still haven't been able to speak. I'm too shocked. I get it now why Jeff's been so cold and acting weird toward me. He knows the only reason a person like me would go through those doors to the clinic is for one reason. He doesn't know the why of it or the shame I feel every waking moment.

Connor apologizes that he's got to leave when his stop comes up but Jeff promises to call him tomorrow to work out arrangements with his aunt for the shelter. I tell him not to sweat it, that I'm a big city girl now and can handle myself. I can tell Jeff wanted to laugh and I'm sure I would have kicked him in the shins if he had. Instead, I let him get away with rolling his eyes.

Thick, awkward silence fills the harsh rumbling of the subway once Connor gets off. I'm counting stops. We have another three before we can both get off. The silence is killing me.

"Why do you work at the shelter?"

"My parents don't come from money and I like to help out."

What the hell? Does everyone think my mom and I come from money? "Yeah, well I don't come from money, either." I snap at him, pulling my coat tight because it's cold in the subway. I can't help notice that Jeff's not bothered by the lack of heat. Maybe he's pulling a macho thing but somehow I don't think so.

He laughs. "That's not the act your mom plays."

Boy did he get that right. I nod. "Yeah, I know. She likes to make it sound like we've always had money. Not the case. Things are different here." *Sort of.* Some things are the same. A flash of Greg on me causes me to clutch my stomach.

"You want to tell me what happened?"

I look at him. We're sitting side by side on the subway and I realize he means it.

"Can't."

I wait for him to urge me on. When he doesn't I fill in the silence.

"It's not like you think." I can't tell him what happened.

"Does Connor know?"

I laugh. "You've so got that wrong."

This time he looks at me. "You should talk to someone," he says. I notice he's got nice soft brown eyes.

I shake my head. "Don't worry about it. I'm taking care of it."

"Still, you should talk to someone. My sister was raped five years ago—"

"What?" I blurt, my attention totally fixed on him.

"Yeah, we don't talk about it much. She's in therapy. Actually we all are. I started to help out at the shelter over a year ago because I hated feeling helpless. It's working, but things will never be the same." He runs his hands on his jeans like he's nervous with his disclosure.

Boy, did he sum that up right.

"I'm in therapy." Of course I don't talk about the issues really affecting me, but Jeff doesn't need to know that. Or does he?

"Is it helping?"

"No."

"Tell her the truth. Open up. It might help you, Lindsay."

"Why do you sound so grown up all of a sudden?" I'm angry we're having this weird adult-like conversation because game-boy Jeff isn't usually like this. Plus telling my therapists that my step-father rapes me sounds easy but it's not.

I pull up my jacket and start scratching my scars. I don't realize I'm doing it until Jeff grabs my wrist.

"What happened?"

"Nothing." I yank my wrists out of his hold.

This time he laughs. "Yeah, I totally get the nothing. Two years ago I tried to OD, so don't tell me it's nothing. When you want to talk I'll listen."

I feel the hard plastic seat dig into my butt and back. The threat of tears makes me feel weak so I dig my nails into my palms to maintain my composure. "Does Blair know that?"

"Oh, yeah he knows all right." The bitterness in his voice hits me. So that's why Blair always insists his buddy hangs with them. He doesn't trust him.

"You two are real tight, aren't you?" I ask, hoping he'll drop his enquiry into me.

His hand pushes his hair off his forehead. For the first time I notice it's light brown. Funny how I never really looked at him before. He's sort of cute in that quiet way of his. After I just saw him take charge with those two homeless ladies I know underneath that quietness is a boy turning into a man of worth. It makes me like him a bit more knowing he won't be like the Gregs in my world.

"We were tight, but people change." He turns his face from mine to watch the flickering reflection of posters as we speed along to our stop.

At our stop, we both get up and step back into familiar but strangely different territory. Something has changed between us.

"You going back to the clinic?" he asks, the minute we're at street level.

I wish I could say no. I can tell by the plea in his eyes he's waiting and wishing for that answer. Strange how I know that. How is it a ten minute conversation can open a window to a person's soul? I almost wish I hadn't nudged it open. It certainly would make things easier. After all this is my burden. This is my shame.

I notice he's shivering in earnest now, shifting his feet back and forth. His hands dig into his pockets and his wide shoulders hunch together in a feeble attempt for warmth. The temperature must be close to minus five and he's only wearing a plain long-sleeved black shirt. "So?" he asks, probing me for an answer.

All I do is nod.

Chapter 24

Megan

"Will you partner up with me in bio again?"

I turn my head and look around for Rebecca or Krista.

"So?" says Lindsay, pushing the door of my locker out of the way.

I look at her. Really look at her. What gives? All morning I've been walking around feeling as if the weight of my laptop has been resting on my head. I barely slept all weekend because I've been so worried about Mom and scared shitless Lindsay would have blabbed to everyone that I'm in the army.

I shut my locker before I answer. "Sure."

"Great, see you in class." Lindsay darts away, swinging her designer purse over her shoulder. We're back in uniforms but unlike Rebecca or Krista who hike up their plaid skirts way above their knees, Lindsay doesn't. Not even when we're off the campus. The minute we are off campus most girls magically transform into a version of a Britney Spears wannabee. Not me or Lindsay.

Making my way to class I know my head's not in the game. I've got this funny sensation that has settled in my stomach and it has nothing to do with my low calorie diet and a lot to do with the fact that I now totally get the phrase, worried sick. In class I'm thrilled we're not dissecting something. Today's lesson consists of looking at a bunch of slides and identifying them. Easy.

Lindsay's settled onto the lab stool beside me but aside from asking me before class to partner up we haven't said anything. *Awkward much.* I move away from the microscope so she can take a turn examining the slides.

"Did you tell anyone?"

Lindsay jots down something on the piece of paper the teacher provided. "No."

The relief I feel causes me to smile.

"You must think I'm a shit, don't you?"

The question startles me because it is so close to the truth. I did think she'd tell. I expected to be the laughing stock of the school. "Sort of."

"Yeah, well your secret's safe with me."

And yours with me. I don't say it though. Instead I move to the microscope and insert another slide.

"There's only two more days before the play. You coming to the center after school?"

"No. I can't. I'll try to be there later, probably around suppertime, but something's come up." Yeah, that something's called cancer and not only is it eating away at my mom it's killing me. Instantly, I regret thinking that thought and start praying in earnest that won't happen. Then I think I'm being stupid because no prayers of mine ever get answered.

"What?" asks Lindsay.

For a minute I'm tempted to let my guard down. It's on the tip of my tongue to say my mom's got MS and a brain tumor.

"Don't sweat it. You don't have to tell me. I get it. I'll let Peter know you'll be by later. Is there anything I can do to help?"

I shake my head. "Thanks. It's complicated."

Lindsay laughs but not in a funny way. "Yeah, what isn't complicated these days. Listen, I'm not going to pry but you can trust me. I'm not into dishing the dirt."

Forcing myself to put another slide on the microscope, I don't say anything. The temptation to spill the beans is overwhelming but as much as Lindsay says I can trust her, I know I can't.

"Megan Rockwell to the office."

The loud voice over the intercom feels like someone knifed me straight through the heart. I start to rearrange the slides back in the box.

"I've got this. You go."

"Thanks," I say to Lindsay. My hands are shaking as I pack up my stuff. A dozen horrible things are going through my mind.

Lindsay helps me stuff my laptop back into its case. "Let me know if you can't come to the center so I can let Peter know and he won't freak out on you, okay."

Why is Lindsay being so nice to me? I sniffle.

"I'm sure it's okay. I wouldn't get so worried about being

called to the office. It's probably nothing."

"Yeah, you're right," I mumble, praying she's right. Taking a deep breath, I hike my stuff over my shoulder. I don't have a fancy purse. My stuff all goes in a thrift-store backpack. At least the zipper isn't broken on this one.

Walking quick and silent through the overly clean halls my hand is on the door knob before I realize there's someone to the side of the office.

"Why didn't you tell me?"

"Johnnie?"

He moves closer to me. His eyes look as tired as mine feel. He didn't come back to the apartment and while part of me was glad, there was another part of me that wished he had. As small as our apartment is, it felt huge without Mom.

"Why didn't you tell me about this place?"

"You left, remember?"

"Yeah, but I went to your old school looking for you."

This time it's my feet bridging the gap. "Why are you here?"

His hand weaves through his hair. "The doctor called my cell and he wants us to come in."

My knees start to shake and if Johnnie hadn't grabbed me I would have landed on the over-polished floor.

"What do you think he wants?" My voice sounds like a frog crawled down it.

"Nothing good." Johnnie urges me back to my feet. "Come on, we had better hustle. Took me long enough to track you down."

Shit. "Sorry about that—"

The shrill bell interrupts me. This time it's me grabbing Johnnie, pushing him to the left of the door.

He shrugs me off. "Wait a sec. Your Principal wants to see you first."

"Did you tell her?"

"Sort of had to. Took me ten minutes to explain who I was. Guess you failed to write my name down for their records. My community college ID came in handy after all."

All the girls moving close to us eye my brother. He's not oblivious to them. He smiles at a few of them and then says he'll wait outside for me. I nod and make my way into the Magistrate's office. On day one she informed me she's not like a school principal she's a magistrate. *Whatever*. Different word. Same meaning.

"Do come in Megan. Please have a seat."

Now that's never a good thing. I sit down in the brown leather chair and a flash of my old school's Principal's office hits me. There the walls were white but stained with scuff marks, not a plant insight, and the old computer was about as large and awkward as the banana boxes that house fruit and vegetables at the food bank. Here, I'm sitting across from an old but elegant mahogany desk. It's got a sleek new top of the line Ipad sitting on it and three green thriving plants including a large fern encompass the spacious room.

A few minutes later after all the nice, polite things are explained, I'm out the door.

"Is that your brother, Megan?" asks Lindsay.

"What?" I say, thinking there is no way she could have seen him because he went outside and I never told her I had a brother. After he left I wasn't sure I had one anymore.

"Megan, come on," says Johnnie, poking his head around the corner. He flashes a smile at Lindsay who turns a shade of pink reminding me of the Luscious lipstick brand she gave me from our makeover night. That night feels like a lifetime ago, not three weeks.

Johnnie moves forward and introduces himself. It's too adult-like for me to get my head around.

"Lindsay," says Lindsay, making me feel foolish for not introducing her.

"Oh, here, Megan. I jotted down the info from the other slides. We're having a test tomorrow on it. Thought you might need them."

Why the tears come then, I have no idea. I nod at Lindsay and attempt to pull it together. In my right hand is the name of a specialist the Magistrate highly recommends. Too many people being nice to me today is my undoing.

Without a word, Lindsay walks forward and shocks the hell out of me by hugging me. My arms wrap around her skinny body but it's her that's giving me strength. She lets go of me.

"Call me if you need anything."

"Thanks," I say, turning before the tears fall in earnest.

"Thanks," says Johnnie, looking at Lindsay not me.

Together, Johnnie and I leave. I feel like a door is being closed…like something terrible awaits me. Then I recall Lindsay's hug. Three weeks ago you couldn't have paid her to do that to me. Change isn't always bad, I think.

I get into Johnnie's red Porsche without a word.

Johnnie starts the engine and shifts into gear with ease. Johnnie always did like cars. "She a friend or something?"

"Yeah, I think she is." I settle into the car, wishing we were going anywhere else but the hospital.

I don't remember much of the drive to the hospital. Johnnie leads the charge inside. At the front he tells the person behind the desk that the doctor called him. She tells us to wait in the waiting room, but this time it's full. Both Johnnie and I end up standing, leaning our backs against the wall. Five minutes later a lady comes out calling out my mom's last name. She butchers the pronunciation of it like a bad weed-whacker. It takes me a minute to realize she's looking for us. We step forward and she smiles, but it doesn't reach her eyes. Funny how I notice things like that now. The hospital is filled with fakes. Then again maybe that's a prerequisite to working here. Bad news can't be brokered with a smiling face.

The lady, who introduces herself as an assistant to the doctor ushers us into an examination room. Johnnie immediately sits on the examination table. I stick to the plastic chair. Plastic after all is safe. A few minutes later in walks the doctor. He doesn't say anything until he's settled into the other plastic chair.

"Thanks for coming. There's been another complication," he says.

Johnnie slides off the examination table and stands next to me. The doctor starts to talk in earnest. I'm trying hard to concentrate but by the time he's done I'm shaking mad. My glance slides up to Johnnie. He's mad too.

"Wait a sec. You're basically saying your recent MRI shows another spot in her brain filled with cancer. Can't you fix it?"

"I'm afraid fixing it will do more damage. I explained all this to your mother earlier and she's requested, like I just explained, that we are not to do anything further."

"I don't get it," says Johnnie.

I get up. “Has she signed papers?” My heart’s beating a slow thud and my brain’s feeling fuzzy. I make a mental note to find something to eat later.

The doctor slowly nods.

I can’t believe she did that. I won’t believe it until I see her.

“We need to speak with her,” says Johnnie, pleasing me, for once taking charge at the right time.

“Certainly. Follow me,” says the doctor.

We’re walking down the hall and only once we’re inside the elevator does the doctor speak again. “This was not a decision your mother made lightly”

Who the hell does he think he is? A prophet or something? He doesn’t know my mother and he certainly doesn’t understand our lives.

“What are you saying?” asks Johnnie.

We pass the third floor and the red light moves to the fourth button. I notice gray scuff marks on the elevator floor.

“I’m saying she’s thought about this a lot. She’s got MS and with the cancer spreading…”

“I thought you said you took it all out,” I state.

“We took out what we found but the MRI shows that the cancer has progressed to more areas of her brain.”

“But you can get that out also, right?” I watch the red elevator light move to the fifth number. The bell rings and we get off the sixth floor.

“This decision is your mother’s. She knows that there’s less than a thirty percent chance she’ll recover fully if we go in again. She also knows even if she survives brain surgery again she’ll have to undergo intense radiation and chemotherapy. No one makes the decision she did today without really thinking about the consequences. Please keep in mind this is her life we are talking about.”

No, it’s my life. Without my mom, I’ll never be the same. By the time I enter Mom’s hospital room, I’m crying. Johnnie pulls me into him and I let him. We move to Mom’s bed. She doesn’t have a private room and there are four other ladies, all with different reasons for being in the hospital dorm-like room. Johnnie parts the white curtain and then I see her for the first time since she had surgery. A large white bandage covers her head, her index finger is hooked up to a monitor and there are other tubes connected to more beeping machines. She attempts to smile but falters.

"Mom." I rush to her side, and carefully lean on her, making sure not to put my full weight on her. I want to ask her why she signed those damn papers. I want to rant at her that she can fight…that she needs to fight, but when I look into her light hazel-colored eyes I notice the black circles under them. She's had them for years but at that moment it's like I notice them for the first time. The doctor's words haunt me. I know now she's stronger than me because she did what I could never do. The doctor was right—it wasn't a decision she made lightly. But while she now might have some peace of mind, I don't.

None of this is fair. "It's okay Mom. We understand." I slide a glance at Johnnie, noting how tense his face is. I might understand her reasons but the selfish me is screaming inside, wanting to beg her to fight for me. For Johnnie. For us.

Johnnie moves to the other side of the bed. Gently he strokes her hand. "We're here for you, Mom. You're going to be okay."

She blinks. I notice the IV fluid dripping into her veins. Mom's eyelids go half-mast. We hold her hand until the meds take full effect, forcing her into sleep. She looks younger and peaceful and I'm hoping that when death finally does come to claim her it will be like this.

One drip at a time.

Silent but eerily peaceful.

Chapter 25

Lindsay

"Ashanti, you are doing great." I'm screaming in glee at Ashanti thinking she will be a star one day. That is if she can find a way out of where she's living. The bruises have healed and with her cinnamon coloring she is back to her beautiful, perky self. She rocks in the Dorothy costume someone in her family made her. The fact it looks more like a Mrs. Claus outfit doesn't hurt the play or the season. Peter's rewrite of the famous Wizard of Oz into a Holiday special is actually good. Who would have thought Peter could write a play?

"George, you need to keep to the left when we do this scene." The minute I say that George stumbles and falls onto the stage, grabbing Ashanti in the process. Laughing, she helps him up. That's the thing with Ashanti, as hard as her life is, she's a trooper. She flashes that toothy smile that makes her shine while pointing George to where he's supposed to be on stage.

"They are fabulous. You all are. But you are the best." Peter drapes his arm around me. I shrug him off.

"Stop that," I tell him. He laughs. Nothing's changed there. Peter likes to flirt with me but I've told him a thousand times it's never going to happen. Like Connor he understands and damn if that doesn't make me like them both a lot more.

"Tomorrow night is the night."

Peter's almost bouncing on the spot. My stomach muscles clench anxiously.

"Do you really think they're ready?" My eyes are on Peter but I'm listening to Ashanti get everyone ready for the next set. Even if we're not ready that little girl twirling like a hula hoop is more than able to tackle this play.

"Yeah, they are. I have to say thank you. I know I coerced you and Megan into helping but I couldn't have done it without your help. You made them come to life on stage and Megan made the stage a reality. I've plastered the area with the posters and I'm praying the ten dollar ticket will enable us to raise enough money to keep this place going for a bit longer. The kids here really need this."

I get that now. "Yeah, you're right. And Peter, you are amazing. I never thought I'd say that but I get now why you do this."

"Gee, thanks. You're going to make me cry if you keep that up. How about a kiss for all my good deeds?"

"Think again." Laughing, I step away from him to walk over to where Megan's working. She's painting a forest scene on the third backdrop. Once again it's stunning. "That looks great."

"Thanks. The kids look great up on stage. That is if George is supposed to fall down every time you do that scene."

Chuckling, I squat down next to her. "I've tried to show him how to move on stage but honestly with tomorrow being opening night we might as well keep that move of his in the script."

This time Megan laughs. "Get that. Sorry again I was late and thanks for helping out earlier. It helped that when I came in the kids had all the paper and paints out and ready to go."

"No problem. I think it helped that you had sketched out the scene for them, actually. They seemed pretty self-sufficient and knew where all the supplies were."

Megan ducks her head back to her work, but I know she's surprised and pleased by my comments.

"Listen, can I ask a favor?"

Standing and dusting off her hands on her worn jeans, Megan says, "Sure."

I've got that nervous feeling invading me again. "I've got to leave early. Do you mind making sure they put all the props away?"

"Yeah, not a problem. I don't need to rush home anyway."

Megan squats down and resumes painting the tree trunk. This morning her brother came to the school but she's acting like it was nothing. I got the distinct impression it was a major something. However, I'm all into respecting someone's privacy.

"Thanks. Peter wanted me to remind you that we're to be here at five tomorrow. Actually, I'm going to come here after school to get things ready. I think these last-minute jitters are going to kill me."

"I can't come earlier but I'll be here around five. I really hope we get a good turn out."

"Me too. After all the work Peter put in to this production it would kill him if it flopped." Honestly, it might just kill me.

"It's a shame he wasn't able to get a major sponsor to help headline the production or something," says Megan.

"What?"

"He said he couldn't get a major sponsor," says Megan, giving me a weird look. I've got this idea brewing in my head and I'm not sure it's a good one.

Megan puts her brush down and stands up again, like she's reading what's going on in my mind. "What are you thinking?"

I smile. "Not sure yet, but I might know of a sponsor. I'm not going to say anything though in case it doesn't pan out."

Megan gives me one of her rare 'you are wonderful smiles'. The last time I saw it was makeover night when she let me paint her face with makeup. I'm not wonderful. The only reason she came to my house in the first place was because I needed a shield. I think she knows that, but like her, some secrets are best kept that way—in the vault.

"I hope you can swing that, because this place means a lot to Peter. You know, I don't get it though. His family's filthy rich and all so why hasn't he approached them for money?"

"Pride, maybe," I say, wondering about what Megan says. "You know, you're right though. I think we should ask him."

"Let's wait until we see how things go opening night. He's got a lot on his mind at the moment and I really don't want to jinx things," says Megan.

"You're right. Listen, I've got to leave but I'll talk to you tomorrow at school if I can get a sponsor, okay?"

Outside, I retie my scarf around my neck. It's six o'clock and I've got twenty minutes to make my appointment. Thinking about it makes me sweat and even though it's minus ten outside I'm hot. It's already Monday so this is my second consultation. When I first went to the abortion clinic I had hoped it would be a quick in and out thing. Turns out it's not. They are thorough and won't proceed with anything surgically until the patient has had two sessions.

Beside the initial appointment with a nurse, tonight I'm meeting with a psychiatrist who according to them specializes in these issues. It had been on the tip of my tongue to say I don't have issues, just one problem that's growing bigger by the day. The truth of it is, they took one look at the near-death scars on my wrists and I got penciled in for the extra-special care. The only thing I want tonight is to get inked in for the procedure. Getting rid of this growth is essential. It's not a choice.

I will never get used to riding the subway. Every time I walk down the stairs leading to the tunnels I feel homesick for Halifax. It must be the juxtaposition. In Halifax the biggest thing transporting people are the extra-long buses. When I rode those I always stood in the section that twists around like an accordion and it used to feel like an adventure. Plus being able to see where you're going is something I like. Riding the subway not so much. For one the windows reveal an underground concrete world filled with graffiti and grime, and secondly ever since Megan pointed out the filth to me the area stinks of homelessness and poverty. Something sticks to the bottom of my boot. Feeling like the grime of the city wants to be glued to me for good, I ignore the squishy-gooey mess spreading across the bottom of the sole of my right boot. When I get home I'm throwing these designer things in the garbage. As long as she doesn't spot them in the trash I'm good to go.

I get off at my spot, walk up the stairs that lead to the street and take a breath in, expecting it to make me feel better. Car exhaust greets me, making me gag. My entire body feels wired but my stomach feels like there's a blender mixing up spaghetti. Bile rises up and I have to force my feet to move across the street to the clinic. The building is innocent looking and nothing on it makes it stand out. It's boring on purpose. If the anti-abortion activists and those religious lifers knew where the nasty went down they'd have pickets flying high declaring me a murderer.

Yeah, screw that. No one protected my innocence but at least I have a choice.

Chapter 26

Megan

My palms are beyond sweaty and I've got the twitches from eating nothing but expired chocolate bars Peter found in one of the boxes in the back room. Death by chocolate actually has a nice ring to it.

I can't stop thinking about death now that I know my mom's days are counted. But being here is better than being at home. I can't stand how alone the apartment feels without Mom.

The rec center has been totally transformed thanks to my works of art and Peter's handy-dandy glue gun. Who knew he could pull of this miracle.

"So, what do you think?" Peter asks the question but he keeps poking his head out of the side curtain to watch the place fill up.

"I think you did a great job." I haul him back in. I still get nervous around him because he's so good looking but we've developed a nice friendly relationship that makes it easier for me to talk with him. Normally, I'd be blushing like mad and noticing my worn sneaks. Not tonight. Plus, I ditched the sneakers and dressed up for the occasion. I might not be wearing some sweet black designer dress with a neat fashionable label but according to Johnnie, I rock this outfit.

I smooth down the tight black dress I picked up at the Salvation Army for fifteen dollars. It means I'll have to find cheaper winter boots than what I had budgeted for, but I couldn't pass the dress up. It's jet black, looks like it's never been worn and has cute little gold buttons down the front with buttons on the side. The best part with the find was it came in my size, seven, which is almost unheard of for me.

"You look amazing," says Peter.

I flash a smile at him. "Thanks." I dart a look at the crew getting ready behind me. Lindsay has her hands full as she shushes the kids to keep quiet. It's sort of like watching a new Sergeant-at-Arms take control of our group. Funny, in its own way. "Think I'll help her out."

"I think she'd like that. I'm going to go to the front and relieve the ticket taker before she tries to walk away with the proceeds of the night," says Peter, attempting to maneuver between the overly-excited kids.

"Just who is the ticker taker?"

"Ashanti's sister, Carmen. I mentioned to Ashanti I needed someone and I think she roped her older sister into helping. I couldn't very well say no when she showed up tonight to help especially since Ashanti's so excited she's here to see her, but to be on the safe side, I had better hustle."

"Are her parents here?" I'm cringing. The idea of either one of Ashanti's parents being here tonight when I know what goes on in that household evaporates my good mood.

"Don't think so. I got the impression Carmen feels the same way we all do. Ashanti told me she stays with her mom's sister most of the time."

"Probably because it's safer for her."

Peter looks at me and nods. "Yeah, you're probably right. I'll touch base at the intermission, okay?"

I nod, watching him weave his way from back stage to the front.

"Can I help with anything?" I ask Lindsay. She's reapplying a kid's face paint without much help. "Here, let me do that." I take the brush from her hand before she can protest.

"Thanks. The kids are sweating so much the paint is coming off already," she says, grabbing George who looks like he's about to puke his guts out.

"George, take a deep breath. You're going to be okay," she says, calmly taking control of the hyper-ventilating kid. "You sure you don't mind tackling their faces?"

Even if I did mind, I wouldn't say that. Lindsay looks totally panicked in a way I understand but thankfully the kids are oblivious. "I'm good. If I need you I'll holler."

"You are a lifesaver. Thanks." She darts away with George in tow to make her way to the front of the line.

I fix the paint on three other kids and then it's curtain time. My heart's racing like I've had six cups of java but I haven't had one all day. Watching the kids parade out onto the stage I find myself standing next to Lindsay.

"They're going to be great," I whisper.

"I can't believe how many people came," she says. "Peter's going to be thrilled. I'm sure with tonight's full performance we'll bring in enough money to keep this place going for a bit."

"That reminds me, did you get a sponsor?"

Closing the curtain, Lindsay says, "Yeah, I did. She's the lady in the front row. I had Peter put aside two rows for her and her clients."

"Okay, the suspense is killing me. Who is it?"

Lindsay gives a soft chuckle. "It's the interior designer my mom hired to do my room. She had mentioned a week ago that every year her company donates to the local shelters so I thought she might be into sponsoring something like this."

Something like this. Yeah, these kids scream shelter and food bank big time. I'm impressed. I'm about to say something when Lindsay grabs my arm.

"Come on. I've got the best seats in the house to watch the performance."

The next thing I know I find myself being hauled from behind the stage to a side door. "What's in there?"

"Found this the other day. It takes us up another level. I know, I didn't think the place had one either. However, it's at the top of the stage. There's not a lot of room but there's a small platform we can sit on and watch. No dangling your feet though because if people look up they might spot us."

I nod at her, thinking she's nuts. The idea of sitting on a small platform that overhangs the stage does not interest me. "Why don't we just sit where everyone else is sitting?"

"You can't be serious." Lindsay turns and looks at me. "You're not afraid of heights, are you?"

"Hell no. It just seems unnecessary."

"Come on. It's a great place to watch."

I don't bother to continue to argue with her. Instead I climb up the ladder and crawl onto the platform. She wasn't kidding. It is small. The platform is about five feet wide and six feet long. We sit and watch. My feet are bunched up underneath my knees just like Lindsay's. However, I'm anything but relaxed. This might be a yoga pose for Lindsay but within a minute I'm having serious leg cramps. *At intermission, I'm crawling down and not coming back up, plus what's the point of me getting dressed up if no one will see me?*

"That dress is gorgeous," says Lindsay.

"Thanks. You look great too." As usual she does. She's got four inch black heels on and she's wearing a navy satin dress that clings to her model figure.

"Yeah, well this dress is killing me. It's too tight."

Since I know the tightness has nothing to do with her eating habits and a lot to do with what's growing inside her, I remain silent. The next thing you know I find myself getting caught up in the play. I'm not sure how long we simply sat there and watched, but after a while I realized Lindsay was crying.

"What's wrong?"

"Nothing." She gives a soft sniffle. I bet the purse draped over her arm doesn't have a tissue. I reach inside my black purse, which is actually Mom's and hand her one. Mom always keeps tissues in her purse and since I didn't bother to empty it for the night, I'm in luck. Or in this case, Lindsay's in luck.

"Why does life have to be so hard?"

Shit, that's the last thing I expect her to say. I plastered on my happy face the minute I walked into the rec center, vowing to get through the night. I don't want to think about how bad my life is and having Lindsay throw it in my face is not helping.

"I know. It sucks."

"That would be an understatement. You know what kills me?"

Silently I urge her on.

"I thought I had it all figured out. I thought it was my choice. I thought I could do it."

"Do what?" I already know what she's talking about, but if we're into dishing and telling secrets she's going to have to spill first.

Lindsay turns her head to look at me. She must be wearing expensive makeup because the only thing out of place on her made-up face is her red eyes. Everything else still looks perfect. I don't know why that angers me, but it does. *Oh, I know why, because nothing in my life has been or will ever be perfect.*

"Can you keep a secret?"

I scoff at her like she's nuts. "Yeah, trust me. I keep secrets."

"No, seriously, this is not funny," says Lindsay.

"Lindsay, nothing in my life has been or will ever be funny so believe me, I get keeping secrets."

I'm not sure if it's the words or my tone of voice that finally convince her, but a minute later out comes her story.

I've got a dozen swear words roaring around in my head, but I bite my tongue and refrain myself.

"I'm disgusting, aren't I?" She's gulping in great big mouthfuls of air.

"Jesus, Lindsay, you aren't disgusting. Your step-father is the disgusting prick and so is your mom. You've got to tell her."

"I can't. She thinks I'm after Greg because of all the lies he's told her over the years."

I reach across the small space and grab her right wrist, turning it up so I can clearly see her scars. "This is not a lie. What you tried to do is real. You need to have it out with your mom. Christ, you tried to kill yourself."

"She really won't believe me. She's jealous of me." She attempts to laugh but fails. "She sent me to a psychiatrist so I could talk to her about my issues but when we drove up to the house she told me not to talk about what I did. What mother says that?"

One on crack, I think.

"Then leave," I say, meaning it. "I get that your so-called perfect life has been far from that but you've got to take ownership of this. Letting your step-father molest you because you don't want to deal with your mom's inferiority complex is shit. Get with the program Lindsay, life sucks."

I know those weren't the kind-support words she expected to hear but I've got bigger things happening in my life. Plus, as much as I'm trying to put myself in her shoes, I can't.

"Yeah, the worst part is I'm pregnant."

"No," I say.

She blinks in surprise at my authoritative voice.

"The worst part is you haven't left already. So what, you're pregnant. At my old school that was the norm. It's not like you're dying or anything. You've got choices."

"Like what?" She's getting defensive but if anger gets her to straighten her spine I'm all for pushing those buttons.

"Lindsay, there are tons of places that can offer you help if you really want it."

"Yeah, that's what the nurses at the clinic told me yesterday."

"Clinic?" I ask.

"I went to an abortion clinic the other day. Actually I've been there twice and my next appointment is next week."

"Is that what you want?"

She shakes her head. "Honestly, at first yes, but tonight, watching these kids and seeing all the young mothers in the crowd beaming with pride at their kids up on stage, I'm wondering."

"Wondering what?"

She flicks her hair off her shoulder. "Just wondering what it would be like if I kept it."

"I can't really tell you what it would be like but I know it wouldn't be easy. Raising a baby is hard work. Seems to me first you need to take charge of this situation. You and your mom need to talk."

"I don't want to talk to her about this."

"Well, if you've already made up your mind."

"But I haven't. I just can't deal with her."

"At least you've got your mom," I say, feeling the weight of my own circumstances.

"Megan, what's wrong?"

This time it's me reaching inside Mom's purse for a tissue. "My mom's got MS and she's got an inoperable brain tumor. She's dying."

"Oh my god. I'm so sorry. I had no idea. Is that why your brother came to the school?"

I nod, finding it hard to talk. The next thing I know Lindsay's arms are around me, holding me tight.

We're both crying in earnest now. My legs are numb and I wish my emotions were.

"You and me, we're a pair," says Lindsay. "You know, Megan, you're my first true friend. And you're right. My life does suck at the moment but I've got choices. I'm really sorry about your mother.

I give a loud sniffle. "You know the worst part of this is that I get why she doesn't want them to operate. She's been fighting MS for a decade and she's in pain every day." I go on to tell Lindsay things about my life I thought I never would. She in turn tells me things about her life that makes me think I've judged her totally wrong. She might be rich but like she said her mom worked her way to the top. And being beautiful has always been something of a curse for her.

I tell her about the scholarship to the Prep school and my goal to become a doctor but I don't tell her about the level of poverty I live in. That I know she'd never understand. I do tell her about my old friends and how my old school created a daycare so that the teens could continue on with their high school education without worrying about their kids all day.

At intermission we both make our way down the ladder. At the bottom we look at each and then give each other a big hug.

"I've got to sort this out but you're right, Megan."

"I am?" I'm rarely right, so I'm thinking she's probably wrong.

"I'm going to talk with my mom. We're going to have it out and as sick as that makes me feel, she needs to know what's been going on." Her hand automatically slides to her stomach.

"So about the clinic?"

"Not sure yet. I've got another week to make my decision," she says.

I look at her and nod. I'm trying to think of something to say but nothing comes to mind.

"You going to continue going to school while your mom's in the hospital?" she asks.

"Yeah I am. She's insisting actually."

"You're lucky your mom cares so much about you."

After listening to her story, I know I am. "Thanks. I love my mom like you wouldn't believe...and the thought of her not being there for me...well, I'm trying not to go there."

"I get that. Honestly, I wish I could say my mom and I have that type of relationship but it's always been much more complicated than that."

We emerge from the small space and make our way backstage. The kids are asking a dozen questions. Lindsay kneels to smooth out part of Ashanti's costume. Watching her interact with the kids I realize she's a natural without even knowing it. But whatever choice she makes is her choice.

I hope her mom understands and kicks Greg out on his ass immediately. More importantly, I hope she isn't the bitch Lindsay portrayed her to be.

Chapter 27

Lindsay

I feel high and low all at once. Telling Megan what's been going on in my life makes me breathe easier. The concert also rocked, which totally surprised us all. The kids were great and Ashanti beamed like I knew she would on stage. Mark my words, that gal's going somewhere. It's really late by the time I get home. I purposefully stayed behind to help clean up. Plus, I wanted to find out if we cleared enough money to keep the rec center going. And we did. The concert brought in over eight thousand dollars, and that combined with the major sponsorship from my interior designer, who loved the play, gave us a total of over thirty thousand. Plus, my mother's designer turned out to be a real trooper. She brought along two local politicians with her and has promised to talk to them about full-time financial contributions to the center. I think the looming city election will help our cause. Wait a sec, it's not my cause. It's Peter's.

I trudge up my steps. The outside lights are still on, lighting my way home. I can't help thinking about the center. Working with those kids changed me. Having Megan enter my life also changed me. All of it in a good way.

The door gets yanked open. My mother's arms are crossed over her chest. It's her famous 'I'm pissed' pose.

"Where have you been?"

"Nice to see you too, Mother." I march into the house feeling like a stranger. I wish my mother and I had the type of relationship that Megan has with her mom.

She grabs my arm, forcing me to a halt. I shake out of her hold. "I left a note on the side table and told Greg I'd be out late."

"Here's what I don't appreciate Lindsay…"

I try not to groan. I'm totally beat and not up to one of her long lectures. "Mother, seriously can we save this for another time?"

"No we can't. You, my girl, will listen. One, why didn't you tell me about the work you've been doing at the rec center? Don't give me that look. I found out all about it through the interior designer I hired who gushed about all your hard work and how proud I must be of you. Proud…only if I knew about it. Why didn't you tell me?"

I start to chew on my bottom lip. There's so much I don't tell her that honestly it didn't enter my mind. "Sorry," I mumble.

"And, two, you left your phone behind and a call came in for you from a clinic saying they had to reschedule your appointment."

Okay, that queasy feeling in my stomach comes back in a mad rush. I gulp, trying to think of what to say.

"What's going on, Lindsay? And I want the truth for once."

I laugh. Can't help it. She's got to be kidding me. The truth for once. I tried for truth a long time ago and look where that got me—shipped off to Toronto, plastic surgery in Mexico and a whole new persona I was supposed to adopt so she, not me, could fit in. She's now glaring at me. I want to glare back but can't. I'm totally wiped. I feel the tears I hate start to form and choke them back.

"I'm still waiting," she says, like I'm one of her employees who sadly disappointed her. I'm not someone she owns, she just thinks that's how our relationship is.

I move into the kitchen, get a glass of cold water and plunk myself down in a chair. I notice instantly the case of opened beer bottles. Great. Greg's been drinking again, oh lucky me. Mom sits across from me. She's still got that expectant look on her face. I know whatever I say will disappoint so I decide right there and then to go for the truth.

"I'm pregnant."

The silence in the kitchen grows thick and evil like black mold. I continue to sip my water and wait for her move. When she doesn't play her cards instantly, I lean across the table so I'm closer to her. Then I decide before she can re-launch her lecture to tell the real truth.

"Did you hear me Mother? I'm pregnant. You might want to thank your husband for this because he's the one who put it there."

The smack is lightning fast and damn if it doesn't hurt. Still I hold the tears back. "Yeah, I tried to tell you before in Halifax what that pervert has been doing to me. Here, see these Mother?" I stick out my wrists so they're in her face and ensure she sees the faint lines. For once I wish I still had the ugly red welts but thanks to her money and the quick trip to Mexico, the truth of what I did has faded. Well, that's her thinking, not mine. "You think I had a choice in this, you are wrong."

I want to screech the words at her, but don't. My words are whisper soft but the potency of them hits her like an earthquake. I watch it all happen. My mother, who rarely loses control crumples before my eyes. Her hands hide her face but the tears start to fall in earnest. I don't offer any apologies because she deserves this. I tried to tell her before many times but she wouldn't listen. The truth is ugly. I get that.

Then she leans across the table, grabs my arms in a soft hold and pulls me onto her lap and my tears fall in earnest. I feel like I'm five years old and just fell off my bike. When that happened she always held me tight while whispering into my hair it would be all right, she'd take care of the scrapes, she'd take of me. Truth is, as I let her hands hold me again, this is exactly what I needed. We're both crying for two different reasons. Her hand soothes my hair but I'm not relaxed. We went down this road once before. I've got the scars to prove it.

"It's going to be okay, Lindsay," says my mother, speaking directly into my hair.

I nod. Speech is beyond me at the moment. I'm waiting for her to set the rules. That's what she did the last time. She said it would be okay but then the list of how we're going to handle everything hit me and I realized then my okay really meant her okay. Finally, once I get control of the tears I turn so I can watch her face. I'm still sitting on her lap and usually she's quick to usher me off. Not tonight. I'm hoping that's a sign of good things to come.

"So you believe me, right?"

The nod is so small I almost missed it. But I didn't.

"I'll take care of this. Don't you worry, I won't fail you again." This time her words are whisper soft.

Those damn tears of mine start to fall again and I'm wondering if that's hormonal because of the pregnancy or because of what she admitted. She failed. Not me. The relief of those words from her lipstick-red lips releases my tension. I slide off her lap and stand.

She follows suit. We're both standing and since we're almost the exact height I can't help notice how awful we look. A small crack of a smile forms on my face and then hers. Then she's hugging me. It's a real motherly hug. The first one in such a long time that I don't want her to ever let me go. She's the one who releases me. I step back, feeling like the weight of the world has been lifted.

"You go up to bed. Tomorrow things will be different. Trust me," she says, sniffling a little.

I nod, but my eyes spot the opened liquor and I've got to wonder why she isn't angry.

"Is Greg here?"

"No," she says. Then it hits me. She already had it out with him. She put two and two together with the clinic call. I smile for real this time. I give her another quick hug and then head upstairs to bed. I'm optimistic for once things will be okay for us. With Greg out of the picture things can't get worse. For the first time in a long time I feel relaxed as I get into bed. Sleep hits me instantly.

When next I pry my eyes open, I hear voices coming from downstairs. For a second I think I'm dreaming. I hear Greg's voice but that can't be. Hurriedly, I get dressed and lumber downstairs. Bad mistake. The morning nausea hits me halfway down the stairs. I grip the banister and count to five before gaining control of my stomach. I'm sweating like a leech sprayed with salt by the time I get to the kitchen door. I push open the door and instantly want to vomit.

"What the hell is going on?" I demand.

The domestic scene of Mother and Greg sitting side by side, sharing a cup of coffee disgusts me. Greg looks at me. Instantly, I want to hide. Mother-dearest pats the chair next to her, but I don't move. I get it now. She's going to once again handle things the best way for her—not me.

I race back upstairs before she can dig her motherly claws into me once again. I'm not stupid but I had thought after last night's confession she'd be on my side. *Yeah, guess I am the idiot.*

She barges into my room because like most things in this house I don't have privacy. No locks for Lindsay because of the 'incident'. I'm throwing clothes into a large suitcase without any thought except escape. Mother sits down on the bed and launches into how best to handle this situation. To say I'm dumbfounded would be an understatement. Her ideal way of handling this is for the "family" to go on an extended vacation to Europe, me have the baby and we'd all return back to Toronto with baby in tow so she and Greg could claim my baby as theirs. Is she freaking kidding me? We don't live in the fifties. Does she honestly expect me to agree to this plan? For a second I stop packing so I can thoroughly look at her. Yup, this is how she wants her master plan to unfold. Once again I don't figure in the equation.

"So let me get this straight." I pause, trying to compose my thoughts. She waits. I can see it in her eyes she expects me to go along with this. After all, her last words said what else could I do. Megan's words come back to haunt me. Choices. I've got choices.

Neatly I fold a pair of black pants into the suitcase. I feel calm and collected now that I totally understand her. The word disappointed haunts me. But, like I said to Megan, people don't really change. "If I don't go along with your plan you're kicking me out, right?"

I'm going to force her to say it. I wait. It's a full minute before she speaks again and she's using that tone of voice I hate. All business, but with a degree of pretend understanding she's mastered. It makes the hairs on my neck stand on end.

"Lindsay, honestly I spent a lot of time last night thinking about what's best for you."

Yeah, right.

"And what does Greg think of all of this? Because you do remember he's been the one raping me."

She stands up, smooths down her skirt and gives me a pointed look. I knew saying the rape word would mobilize her. "Don't play all innocent with me. He's told me how you come on to him."

I blink. When the feminist movement hit obviously my mother must have been on another planet. Doesn't she know, no means no. "Believe what you want Mom but I hate Greg. I hate him for what he took from me. What he did to me and for this, but most of all I hate you." I place my hand over my stomach to emphasize my point. "You know I could report him to the police."

"I understand that you hate me right now, But seriously, Lindsay it's your word against his and you're not thinking rationally."

There is nothing rational about this conversation. Knowing she'll back Greg's word over mine makes me want to claw her eyes out. Doesn't matter. I'm out of here. "You don't get it. I never once looked at Greg like you think I do. I hate the very air he breathes. But guess what, Mother? Don't you worry about me. I'm done with you. I'm taking care of me from now on."

She scoffs. "Exactly what is your plan? You're sixteen, you don't work, don't bring in any money, and if you're planning on keeping the baby, how will you manage that all on your own?"

A vivid memory of the concert last night flashes through me. That rec center was half filled with teenage mothers. If they can do it, I can do it.

"Maybe I won't keep it."

"You'll regret that choice all your life if you do that," says Mother.

I continue placing clothes in my suitcase. I know she thinks I'm being dramatic. What she doesn't understand is I'm finally being truthful. "I highly doubt that, but it doesn't matter. The choice is mine."

She moves toward the door with her arms crossed over her chest. I'm glad she's angry. I'm madder than hell.

"Greg and I talked last night and we'd really like to help you."

Okay, I'm the one laughing now. Her and Greg. Not her and me. So much for placing my trust in her to make the right choices for me.

"I can't listen to you anymore. I'm leaving."

"And where are you going to go?"

I click the suitcase close. "You know I'm not sure, but the clinic gave me lots of cards for social workers so I think I'll be okay."

She looks appalled by the thought of me going to a social worker. I get that. Getting a social worker means she'll be exposed. I sense I could negotiate with her but at the moment all I want is out of this house of hell. "I'm going to go to a friend's house for a bit. I can't stay here any longer. Trust me I won't tell anyone what's going on."

I can tell she's about to let me go because I've promised to keep this dirty little secret a secret.

"Please leave me."

The last part comes out sounding like I'm begging and maybe I am. I need her gone. I had a great sleep last night because truthfully, I trusted her. Now, I know that will probably be the last good sleep for me in a long time. I was foolish to think she'd place my needs above her own but not anymore.

I get what motherhood means. She doesn't.

Chapter 28

Megan

The apartment is quiet without my mom and I feel lost. I've tidied up as much as I can just to keep busy. We never had a lot of extra stuff to begin with so finding places for everything turns out to be easy. I barely slept after the concert. Turned out it was a huge success, thanks in part to Lindsay getting her interior designer to sponsor the event. It's Saturday and my stomach is growling. Peter gave us the day off from the rec center but I almost wish he hadn't. There's nothing in the fridge. Just as I'm about to pop out to the food bank, in walks my brother.

"Thought you might be hungry." Johnnie drops a box of Tim Horton's donuts and a coffee on the table. Normally, I'd tell him to get lost but with how things have been lately, I'm not about to pass up free food.

He plunks himself down on the worn sofa. "So, you ready to tell me about that Prep school you go to?"

"Nope." My mouth is almost stuffed full with a chocolate donut which saves me from giving into his question.

I can't help but notice how polished he looks in his designer clothes. Nice to know he's wearing them not because of drug money. The fact my brother got his stuff together gives me hope. "You going into the hospital today?"

Johnnie nods.

"Great. Give me a minute to finish eating and I'll come with you."

He stretches out on the sofa, making himself at home. I realize then this is his place too, but for months that's not how it's felt.

He kicks off his shoes and asks, "So, you're okay with Mom's wishes?"

Okay with them? Yeah, wrong. "No, but what can I say. Hey, Mom I want you to have the brain surgery again because I'm selfish and I want you to live." I stuff a jam-filled donut in my mouth. The strawberry jam takes like heaven.

"That actually sounds good to me," says Johnnie. "I'm not okay with her decision." He takes a sip of his coffee, waiting for me to say something.

"Don't get me wrong, Johnnie, I'm not okay with what's she decided but I think what the doctor said is right. We've got to put ourselves in her shoes. She's been in constant pain for years and now this…I don't know, I'm not sure I have the right to be selfish and ask her to live just for us."

"Why not? For fuck's sake, we're her kids."

"You think she made her decision lightly? Fuck you, Johnnie." Suddenly the donuts feel like lead in my stomach. I get up and grab my purse. "I'm ready. Let's go. And Johnnie, don't you dare say anything to Mom about this. She's made her decision. We're the ones who will have to deal with it."

Johnnie grabs my arm. I try not to cringe but can't hide my reaction. He steps back. His face is flaming red with embarrassment. Things between us will never be normal, I realize, but like accepting Mom's decision, we're going to have to learn to live with each other. When Mom goes, he'll be all I have. I try hard not to think of that because it makes me feel instantly depressed.

"I'm not going to say anything to her, it's just that…"

He stops talking and looks at me. His green eyes look misty. Who would have thought Mr. Tough Guy would get all emotional? Me, that's who. Growing up he was the one who sat with me to watch those stupid Disney movies and when I cried he did too. He always said he had a cold. I got the fact him blowing his nose had nothing to do with his sinuses and a lot to do with how he felt about Bambi losing his mom, but not once did I let on. Maybe our relationship was always pretend.

"It's just not fair," he says, finishing my own thoughts.

"Yeah, I get that, but our life was never fair to begin with so why should this be any different?"

He sighs. "I'm worried about you. I can't…honestly, I don't know what I can do to help when—"

"She dies. Don't worry, things will work out okay." Johnnie gives me one of his pointed looks like he knows I'm full of shit. I open the door and head into the hall because the truth scares the hell out of me and I don't want to talk about it anymore. I have no idea what I'll do when Mom dies and it's a when now, not an if. I realized that last night when I came home that staying here in this empty apartment which had been my home won't last. I'm only fifteen. Once I hit sixteen I can get social assistance but until then Johnnie, my brother, will be my guardian. He and I know I can't stay with him. What he allowed to happen to me is the ugly secret we don't want to acknowledge but like a fake tan it's noticeable.

It takes us half an hour because of the city's traffic to get to the hospital. By now I've got the route down to Mom's room. We're almost at the door to her dorm when one of the nurses rushes around from the nursing station.

This time I grab Johnnie's arm to stop him from opening the door to Mom's room. A sick feeling of dread sweeps through me.

"We tried to reach you," says the nurse to both of us.

It's on the tip of my tongue to tell her the phone got disconnected last week because we couldn't pay the bill which was overdue by two months, but thankfully Johnnie saves me that embarrassment.

"We're here now. What did you want?" I can tell his abrupt tone is not to her liking, but coming to the hospital to visit our dying mother sucks big time.

"Ah, the doctor tried to reach you when your mom had another seizure and…"

I don't realize my hand is gripping Johnnie's arm until he moves closer. Instantly, I let go and take a breath in while I try to compose my thoughts. "And what?"

"I really think the doctor should be the one to tell you," says the nurse. She's darting her eyes to the nurse's station and I realize then they've already called the doctor.

"Tell us what?" asks Johnnie, stepping closer to the now-panicked nurse.

I don't wait for her to speak. Instead, I push open the door and march over to the curtained off area where Mom's been parked. The nurse is still talking about nothing to Johnnie, who followed me into the room. Yanking back the curtain I notice fresh linen is on the bed.

"Where is she?" I turn to face the nurse, but know by the look on her face that the where is not a place I'm going to like.

She straightens her spine and using her best commanding voice says, "I need you both to come with me." Without waiting to see if we are willing to follow her she turns on her heels and this time we're the ones tagging along like obedient puppies. All the gusto I felt flew out the window the minute I yanked open the curtain and found nothing. No Mom. The reality of my worst fear coming to life hits me and I feel like a walking zombie. I glance over at Johnnie. He's biting his lower lip and his head's hung low. We're both placing one foot in front of the other like it requires a concerted effort, so much so we're not speaking and I feel like I'm barely breathing.

The nurse quietly ushers us into a side room. You know instantly this room is designated for one purpose. The walls for one look nice, not scuffed up like the walls in the room Mom occupied and there looks to be a real plant sitting in the corner. No doctor desk, just a round wooden table with four chairs. Both of us sit down. The nurse leaves and twenty seconds later in walks the doctor. I can tell he practically ran all the way to the office because he's slightly winded. We let him adjust his white lab jacket and only once he takes a seat do I find my voice.

"Where is our mother?"

He folds his hands on the table and I blink. I'm fighting not to cry because the only reason we're in this room is for him to officially announce what I've been thinking.

"We tried to reach you earlier. Your mother had two major seizures and I'm sorry…we tried to do as much as we could, but about an hour ago she died."

An hour ago I was eating a donut filled with strawberry jam. I remember feeling guilty because it tasted so good and jam filled donuts were always Mom's favorite. I don't know why I think that but I do.

I wipe my hands on my jeans because I'm starting to feel nauseous. I'm waiting for Johnnie to say something but all he's doing is swiping a hand through his hair.

"Where is she now?"

I can tell my question startles the doctor. He leans back in his chair. "The body is in the morgue but you are welcome to visit."

The thought of visiting the morgue does not sit well with me.

"Megan, we are not going to the morgue."

I'm glad Johnnie's finally found his voice. I nod at him and will the tears not to fall. The doctor gets up and clears his throat. You can tell it's a move he's done a hundred times.

The doctor grabs his white lab coat, drawing it close to himself. "I'll give you a few minutes to absorb everything and when you're done there's some paperwork you will need to fill out."

Johnnie nods. I'm glad for once he's taking charge. My mind is trying to wrap around the notion that my mom's dead. We both watch the doctor leave. Johnnie places his arms on his legs. Me, I'm left looking at the fern.

"So what do we do know?" asks Johnnie.

I give him my 'you have got to be kidding me' look he knows so well. His eyes are red, like he's having a hard time holding it together.

"Yeah, that's what I thought," he says.

"Can you fill out the paperwork? I'm really not up to that."

Again, a nod. Johnnie gets up abruptly, causing the chair to scrape the floor. "Jesus, I'm not ready for this. I thought we'd have more time."

I want to say I thought that too, but deep down, I realized the minute Mom made her decision she gave up the fight. I want to weep, bury my head in the sorrow I should feel for her but instead I'm feeling numb. It's sort of an angry mix coated with a sense of being overwhelmed.

I get up and approach Johnnie. "I'm not staying with you."

"Sort of figured that, but where are you going to go?"

Now that's the big question. Honestly, I don't know. I didn't have time to formulate a plan. "I'll figure it out. I've got the apartment for a few more weeks."

"You going to call the social worker?"

I roll my eyes. He's got to be kidding. Calling the social worker will only lead to questions. Many of which I don't want to answer. Namely, why I don't want to live with my brother.

He stands up and puts his shoulders back. It's a move he used to do when someone was bullying me. He might not have been bigger then but with that determined glare in his eyes and confident march he always scared them off. I know more than anyone else it's his way of coping—his shield that protects him. I so wish I had developed one.

"I'll fill out the paperwork. You staying here?"

Shaking my head, I head for the door. This place, like the fern I had been admiring, is fake. "I'll meet you in the car."

Johnnie hands me the keys and I leave him to fill out all the paperwork. My heart's beating slowly and it's only once I'm in Johnnie's car does it truly hit me. Alone. I'm going to be totally alone. I'm not ready for this. I don't want it. That angry feeling sprouts like a newly planted seedling.

Why couldn't she fight for me…for us? Life isn't fair. Just when I thought I could make it with faking my okay-life at the Prep school, I've got to figure out how to force myself to continue acting the role all on my own. The reality is all I want is my mom, and her tiny frame in the wheelchair as she waits expectantly at the apartment door to hear all about my day. School was a means to escape my situation but now with Mom gone I've got to wonder if it's worth it.

Chapter 29

Lindsay

"I shouldn't have come over." I think that's the third time I've said that sentence in less than five minutes. Megan is a total mess. We both are in fact. When she called me from a pay phone and told me about her mother dying it totally threw me. Then she asked me to come over. Now, as I watch her rock back and forth on the ugliest sofa I have ever seen, I'm wondering if maybe I should have given her more time to grieve, privately.

Megan sniffles loudly and blows her nose again into a tissue. "No. I'm glad you came over. I really don't want to be alone."

"What about your brother? Does he know?"

Megan nods. "We drove to the hospital together this morning and found out. Honestly, I'm not sure where he is now. I asked him to drop me off at the apartment."

I plunk myself next to her on the sofa. "Doesn't he live here too?"

"No. He moved out a few months ago. Now, it's just me and I won't be able to afford this place on my own."

I look around at her apartment. I thought I knew Megan, but that's wrong. My eyes absorb everything and I know she sugar coated her life. Everything in the apartment has come from a thrift store and when I opened the fridge there wasn't any food. How does she live like this? And why didn't she tell me?

This isn't the time to ask those questions, so I keep my thoughts to myself. "How long can you stay here?"

"Two more weeks."

We've got fourteen days to figure out something for her and me. "Look, I'm going to run down to the corner store and get some food. I'll be right back."

Megan practically leaps up off the sofa. "Not a good idea. Give me a minute." Next thing I know she's moving things around in her room only to return with a large, beige sweater. I look up at her. "What's with that?"

"You can't go walking around in this neighborhood wearing what you're wearing."

I can't help but look at myself. Sure I'm wearing designer jeans and a leather jacket but honestly, my clothes aren't that flashy. I wasn't even thinking about fashion, just escape from my mother's sick plan for my life. "You can't be serious."

Megan silently purses her lips together. "Sorry, I am. I'm surprised you didn't get mugged getting here."

I want to argue my case but can tell by the look in Megan's eyes she's dead serious. Without another word I put on the sweater. Together we make our way to the corner. A blush steals over Megan's face.

"I don't have any money."

"No sweat. I do. Let's get some packaged sandwiches, yogurt and chips. It's not much but it's a start to eating our way to feeling better." That gets a twitch of a smile out of her and makes me feel marginally better. As much as I hate my mother at the moment for all she's done to me I can't imagine how I'd cope if she died.

Fifteen minutes later I'm out close to twenty bucks but honestly it's no biggie. I've got close to five thousand in my bank at the moment thanks to my mother's generous allowance program and I know that's a lot more money than Megan thinks I have. Still, as the enormity of our situations kicks in I've got to wonder how long that money will last.

Back at her apartment we stuff our faces first with chips. Later we'll go for the healthy stuff but junk food does soothe the soul.

"So, you left your mom for good?" asks Megan, waiting for me to launch into my story.

I told her briefly over the phone that I had to leave but when I finally got to her apartment she wasn't in any condition to deal with my problems. Ten minutes later my tale is told. To say she's astounded would be an understatement.

"You can't be serious."

I open the blueberry yogurt and eat a spoonful, already regretting my pig-out episode. That nauseous feeling I've become so aware of is starting to hit me. "Oh, yeah, I am. Mother's all about what works best for her. Not me."

"So she wants you to go away and come back and pretend she and Greg had a baby and not you. People won't buy that," says Megan.

I roll my eyes. "Doesn't matter. Nobody will question her. That's the thing with my mother. She knows how to work people and the system to get what she wants."

"But does she really want a baby, knowing how it came about? I just don't get that."

"Spend sixteen years with my mother and you will. Greg is her eye candy. He makes her feel young and she's convinced she's in love with him. What Greg's done to me is irrelevant in the grand scheme of Mother being happy. Forget Lindsay's happiness. I don't equate with what's really important in her life."

Megan gets up and pours water from the sink into two cups. Handing me one, she sits back down. "I think you should call a social worker."

"I could say the same thing to you." We're both looking at each other, reading each other's thoughts.

"Can't," says Megan. Her reasons for not calling aren't my reasons but my gut says they might be pretty damn similar.

Megan eyes the yogurt but instead crumples up the chip bag. I watch her place it in the trash and realize as hard as my life is, Megan's has been harder.

"You're welcome to crash here as long as you like."

Megan's offer is exactly what I needed to hear because I didn't know where else to go. Who would have thought? A few weeks ago I wouldn't have given her the time of day. Now she's become my best friend, in the truest sense of the word. I get up and hug her. For a second she's as stiff as an unripe banana but then she responds, clasping me to her. We stay that way for a long time. Holding on to each other, reassuring each other we'll be okay when the harsh reality is that neither of us knows the outcome.

Slowly we release each other, somewhat reluctant to let go of our hold. "Thanks Megan. We'll work out something together, okay?"

She gives a small nod. It's a start.

"Give me half an hour to clean out Mom's room and then you can crash there."

"I'll help." I take off the sweater and hand it to her.

"No. Thanks. I need to do this alone," says Megan, taking the sweater.

I get that. I nod, and plunk myself back down on the sofa wishing I hadn't forgotten my laptop. As I look around the sparse apartment I realize Megan probably doesn't have Internet, so it doesn't matter. That's what I tell myself, but deep down it does matter, because one way or another I'm going to have to go home and get my laptop all without facing Greg or my mother. Since that's about as likely as free wireless in this rundown apartment complex I'm not holding out hope.

Chapter 30

Megan

Pretending things are normal is supposed to make you feel better. It's not working. I'm glad though I haven't been alone since Mom died. Between Lindsay staying and Johnnie popping over to check in on me I've been somewhat okay. Johnnie playing the doting big brother part actually feels real, but since I'm never all that comfortable with him hanging out in the apartment, he usually leaves after twenty minutes of mostly me being silent while Lindsay tries to carry the conversation. I couldn't believe Lindsay told Johnnie what happened to her. Not exactly sure what her game plan is but I'm surprised she told him her ordeal. A month ago when I suspected what was going on she certainly tried to keep me unaware. I think she knows my brother-sister relationship is not normal but no way am I about to tell her the ugly secret that's totally all Johnnie's fault.

I place my gear in my locker, and just like normal I've got no lunch. For once I'm not fighting my normal hunger pains. Lindsay and I went shopping at a real grocery store. I had no idea she had a credit card. When she laughed about it, I could tell she thought everyone had one. Everyone except me.

I smell Peter's cologne before he gets close to me.

"How you doing?"

Great, Peter knows. I had asked Lindsay not to say anything to anyone, but lately her loose tongue has a way with her.

"Okay." I'm trying to unhook my arms from my sweater. I place my laptop on the floor and finally manage to wrestle free from Lindsay's black cardigan. She actually threw my old sweater in the garbage and only confessed to the crime after I spent an hour looking for it. Since I don't have a lot of clothing I figured she must have done something. Her peace offering was this and it wasn't in me to say no. "Gather Lindsay told you?"

"Yeah, man, I'm real sorry. Why didn't you tell anyone?" There's an accusing tone in Peter's voice I don't like one bit.

"Not my way of coping." My answer is short and I'm about to turn away from Peter when he grabs my arm.

"We're your friends, Megan. We care about you."

I laugh in his face. Can't help it. Friends? He certainly wasn't my friend when he forced me to join his special rec group project. It's on the tip of my tongue to tell him off.

He leans in close, blocking out the people walking through the halls. His lips are mere inches from mine and I'm wondering what the feel of his lips would be like. I will my heart to slow down, knowing I'll never find out.

"Think what you want but we do care about you. I'm here if you need anything. Anything at all." His spearmint breath teases my nose. I look up at him, wishing this wasn't happening now.

I force myself to look down at my black school shoes. Today is uniform day so having to wear the ugly flat shoes is part of the package. Too bad mine are second hand and half a size too small for me. They pinch my toes and by the end of the day the feel of my worn sneakers feels like heaven to my feet. My gaze moves to Peter's black shiny leather loafers. He might care about the kids at the recreational center but his home is still a mansion. Mine is a sorry excuse for an apartment.

"Megan, do you hear me?"

I heard him but I'm having a hard time finding my voice. Lately, I find myself always on the verge of tears. Just how long will I feel like this? On Friday morning my mom was alive. Today is Monday, so it's only been two days of feeling like an orphan but I think this feeling is a keeper for the rest of my life.

He releases his hold on my arm and takes my hand. I'm startled. He gives it a squeeze and then before I can say anything he gives me a quick kiss on the cheek.

"I've wanted to kiss you since the first time I saw you."

There had been a time when those words would have meant everything to me. I'm not so sure they do now. "And when was that?"

"That night when you and Lindsay were drunk on the school steps," he says, fighting a grin.

See, that's the thing with Peter. I've noticed him since day one at this school but it took him months to even see me and the reality is that night he didn't spot me so much as Lindsay. I've always been the afterthought girl.

I force him to let go of my hand. Peter's trying to be nice but I'm not ready for it. "Thanks Peter. I'm not myself. I just need some space. I'm not used to relying on other people." *Because those people always let me down. History learned and hopefully not repeated.*

"Sorry. I just wanted you to know that I really care about you. I'll leave you alone but Megan, if you need anything at any time you call me." He hands me a business card with his cell number on it. How many teenagers in high school have business cards?

I laugh. He blushes.

"Had to get them for the recreational center. I give them out to some of the kids letting them know if they need to reach me to call me."

Jesus Christ is that how he sees me—another special project? I tuck his card inside my binder, planning to chuck it in the garbage later. We part, each dashing to class and the reality of what I'm trying to do floors me. All of these kids here in this school get to go home to their happy family. Me, I get to go home to no one. Okay, Lindsay's there but for how long? She found it hard enough staying with me for the weekend and all her jabs about the used furniture and lack of food are annoying.

Makes me wonder if she thinks money grows on trees. Maybe in her family it does but in mine what money we got only let us live. There was never extra. Never any to put away for a rainy day, like my teacher in our Business class preaches. The first time he said that I knew my reality was no way at all similar to his or to the kids in my class. All of them have bank accounts. Me, what I've got is in my pocket and trust me, the loose change does not amount to much.

Lindsay passes me in the hallway. We sort of parted ways once we hit the school grounds. We both needed some space. She of course did her usual bonding with her girl crew. Funny how she dished the dirt on them all weekend but come Monday morning she walks right up to them like she's part of the "in crowd". Appearances do mean something to her and I'm wondering when she'll let them know her growing secret. I bet she didn't tell Peter that biggie.

"See you in Religion class," she says."

I groan. She laughs.

"Yeah, know exactly what you mean. I hate that class the most. The priest is a pervert," whispers Lindsay.

Since she knows all about perverts I bet she's right. I hate the class for a different reason. Confession. Not once since I started here did I tell the truth during my so-called one on one time with the priest but the urge for once hits me.

I walk into class and take the last seat in the far back row. I get out my laptop and turn it on and then I place my hands under my legs, anchoring them and me in place. I'm hoping by the time class is over that feeling to purge my soul will have evaporated.

Chapter 31

Lindsay

"You coming back to the apartment?" School was torture. I thought for sure Mother would have called the Magistrate and I'd get the call first thing in the morning over the dreaded intercom system. Then it would be me slinking my way to the guidance office. None of that happened. Now the bell's about to ring and there's a part of me that wants to go home. I have to get my laptop. Not having it today for class was a real downer. I actually had to take notes using a pen and paper. How archaic.

Megan's question should be easy to answer. It's not.

"Go home. Come back if you need to. We've got the place until the twenty-seventh, so I'm there if you need me." Megan darts out the school door and then my decision is made. Ah, the joys of going home.

I walk my usual route on automatic. I'm about to open the side door so I can quietly get into the house through the kitchen route, or as Mother likes to say loudly, the servants door. Waiting for me is Greg. By the looks of the used coffee mugs he's been sitting at the kitchen table for a while.

"Thought you'd come home."

"Trust me I wish I wasn't here."

"Yeah, but you forgot this." He kicks my laptop out from under the kitchen table. "Knew you'd come back for that."

"Mother home?" I start to walk past him when he stands up. Greg's tall at a good six foot-four and even though I've got height, he always makes me feel small and dirty. I will him to let me pass untouched, but that's a no-go. He grabs me by the shoulder forcing me to look up at him.

"You planned this, didn't you?"

The word bitch was on the tip of his tongue and we both know it. Leaving this house and being with Megan and seeing how she's coping has changed me. "Yeah, that's right, Greg. I want your bastard child growing inside of me, because if there's one thing missing from my life it's a constant reminder that you raped me night after night." He's so stupid I'm wondering as I spin out of his hold if he'll get my sarcasm.

"You really are a bitch, Lindsay. You had better do what your mother wants or else."

I don't even ask or else what? He wants me to ask but honestly my decision was made the minute I opened that door and saw his sorry excuse of a dog-face. This child will always remind me of him. Having his child will ruin me forever. In my room I stuff another large suitcase full of clothing, half expecting him to storm in. Not like I can stop him because even with my new designer bedroom, I don't have a lock. Fifteen minutes later I've got my stuff, well, all the stuff I care about. I've even packed the one picture I have of Mother and that damn tree we planted in our Halifax backyard.

Lugging the suitcase downstairs I'm greeted with Greg.

"I called your mother."

I laugh. "Seriously, Greg is that your threat. It's 3pm and unless you're dying, which really would make me happy, she's not leaving the office. Trust me when it comes to me, I don't count when it's during working hours and if there's one thing you should know now about Mother-dearest is she's all about her image, work and money. Bye Greg. You and Mother truly do deserve each other."

I can tell by his stunned expression he's shocked at my disclosure. Well, wake up Greg and get with the program.

"So you're leaving for good."

"Looks like that doesn't it."

For the first time he looks sheepish, like's he worried about me. Yeah, right.

"Don't worry, I'm not having it. The thought of your child makes me barf. But you know what Greg?"

He looks at me and I stare back feeling like I've finally found my backbone. "What makes me really sick in all of this is my own mother. You. You're dirt and nothing but a fucking pervert. And don't interrupt me, because once I leave this house I'm never coming back. What gets me is my own mother didn't once believe me, but that's not entirely true. You see, I think she knew all along what was going on but she wanted you…her eye candy guy, she's madly in love with, so much so she's willing to hatch a plan that saves her face while destroying me. These scars…:"

I take a breath and thrust out my arms, whipping up my sweater so my wrists are in his face. "These scars might be faded but they remind me every day how you made me feel. That, more than this baby growing inside of me, is why I'm leaving. I never want to feel like shit again. You and her, you both did that to me. Not anymore."

He snickers. "So, you're going to make a go of it in the real world, Linds. Get a real job, make minimum wage after having all of this." He spreads his arms wide to indicate our grand foyer. I roll my eyes at him.

"You don't get it Greg, I don't care about any of this. These walls might look great with the new décor but they're plaster and wood. This place was never my home. It was a building built on lies, treachery and enough indecent things that Mother-dearest will pay me to keep my mouth shut."

His eyes widen. Ah, I see he finally gets it. Blackmail. Part of me thinks I am a bitch for thinking of doing this to my mother, but the harsh reality is she taught me everything I know. Some behavior might be inherited but sixteen years of living with Mother and I know she'll cough up dough for my own place and more. After all, the last thing she'll want is a scandal that could tarnish her image as the loving, doting, philanthropist mother.

I turn the knob on the front door.

"You planning to take that on the subway or what?" asks Greg.

I turn and face him. "Nope. I called a cab. Tell her I'll be in touch."

I'm out the door before he can respond. A second later the cab pulls up. The cab driver puts my luggage in the back and I know he thinks he's taking me to the airport, but that's not my destination.

"We're to?" he asks.

The minute I give Megan's address he raises his head so he can eye me in the rear view mirror. Maybe it's the look on my face as I say goodbye to what had been my neighborhood, but whatever the cause I'm happy when the cab driver doesn't question me.

Forty-five minutes later he drops me off. I gave him a good tip because I valued the quiet drive. It gave me time to think and by the time I'm at Megan's apartment I've got a plan that will benefit both of us.

I open the door and before I've made it two feet inside, Megan's poking her head out of the apartment door.

"Thought you were staying at your house?"

I pull my large suitcase down the hall and she holds the door as wide as it can go so I bring it inside the apartment. I turn to her and say, "A house is only a home by the people inside of it."

She laughs. "What, you read that on some bumper sticker didn't you."

I laugh also, saying, "Yeah, that's right." It's not.

We're just two young girls trying to cope in the world that's treated us wrong. I've got money, she's got none. I like fashion and she doesn't have a clue about what lipstick to choose but deep down we're suited for each other. Megan's my best friend, my only friend and one I don't plan to ever let slip away.

"I've got a plan for us."

"Hope it's better than what you said in Religion Class," she says, walking pass me. That gets a real laugh out of me.

"What, you didn't think me telling the priest I wanted to convert to Judaism was funny?"

She's plunked herself down on the worn sofa. I sit down beside her. "Oh yeah, only about as funny as me saying I was becoming a Muslim. Thought the old guy was going to have a heart attack. You do know he sent letters to the Magistrate."

"Seriously, like I care. Listen, I've got a plan for us." I lean back, put my feet up on the old wooden coffee table and tell my plan to Megan. By the time I'm done she's looking at me like I'm crazy. I'm not. And trust me, once I talk to Mother, Megan will believe me. She just doesn't know my mother like I do.

"What if she says no?" asks Megan.

"She won't. Will you come with me to the appointment?" That was the other part of the plan. I found that part hard to ask.

Megan leans over and next thing you know we're hugging. "Yeah, I will. I'll be there for you," she says.

"And I for you," I say, meaning it for real.

Then we start to giggle. That's the thing about Megan and me. One minute we're sad and the next we're happy. You might wonder how we can be happy when our lives are so messed up but that's our reality. I want the happy more than I want the scars of that depression I went through. I survived that and now with Megan in my life I will survive this.

Our lives will never be normal but we've got each other and for now that's great. Not perfect. But okay.

About the Author

Renee Pace calls Halifax, Nova Scotia Canada home and loves living by the Atlantic Ocean. Happily married mother of four children, she juggles writing, children's hectic schedules and running a paddling club. Renee enjoys writing nitty gritty and paranormal young adult stories.

Renee is a member of Romance Writers of America, Romance Writers of Atlantic Canada, the Society of Children Writers & Illustrators and the Writers Federation of Nova Scotia.

Renee Pace can be reached at www.reneepace.com or twitter at@ReneePaceYA

If you enjoyed Off Limits, you will also enjoy…

Off Leash

By Renee Pace

Chapter 1

Ollie

I am suffocating inside my plastic lined steel-barred cage, dying with the thickening silence and quiet sobbing coming from the other room. Locked inside for more than half of the day, my body twitches for the feel of the brisk air that causes my drool to freeze to my face.

Big footsteps lumber down the stairs. Instinctively I cower as far back inside my cage as possible, lowering my body to the pee-stained blanket in an attempt to make my big frame small while keeping my eyes downcast. A whine slips from me when he kneels in front of the cage. Is he going to haul me out for a beating? He did it yesterday when I peed.

He stands, glaring at me with eyes full of hatred but then turns away, and just when I think I am in the clear he gives my cage a good hard kick, forcing it to almost roll over. At the last moment, I leap up forcing my legs wide to keep it upright. Task accomplished, I sit back down and wait.

He leaves. The door shuts loudly behind him. I relax.

Head on my paws, I try to sleep. Can't. Standing again, I can barely turn around. My legs are cramping in the too-hot musky cage. Gnawing on the bars is useless. I know that from previous experience, except I'm bored and need to pee again. I know now not to bark. That gets me nowhere.

I start whining in earnest. My paws push at the hard plastic frame. I need to run. Doesn't anyone understand? I need to stretch. I need to get out.

The doorbell rings.

At first I think she is going to ignore it. After all, when he came down the stairs she ignored me and sat like a frightened bird in the other room. The creak of the door opening excites me. She motions for someone to come into the room. A blast of frigid air hits me. I can almost smell freedom. Then the door shuts.

I hear footsteps from the other room as they move to where I'm caged. Hers are familiar because of the soft tread. The other steps are hesitant. My head goes up and my ears perk forward, but curiosity makes me cautious.

I look up. A boy stands in front of my cage. He's shuffling his feet and he looks lost.

When the cage gets unlocked I try hard not to leap out. It's too much. Stuck in that hole for too long, my back leg muscles flex with joy and my front paws jump up, almost pushing her, my owner, over.

A good loud command from her instantly forces my body to freeze. Following her pointed hand motions, I sit. She is all business. If I jump up again I will land back in the cage. Not understanding her words does not mean I don't understand her meaning.

I look at the quiet boy. He's nodding, not speaking. My entire body itches to move. I lower my eyes. I force the stillness. I don't even prance around. She talks fast, using hands to speak to the boy. Thrusting the leash into his hand the boy warily glances at me.

Great, another walker. I know now not to get attached. He might last a day or two with me, if I am lucky. Then he will move on to something easier…something inside where it is warm.

My heart speeds up when he gives a good tug on the leash and moves to the door. He acts all business-like, but the scent of his excitement, like the cool air now coming in from the slightly opened door is refreshing. We shall see who runs who.

Chapter 2

Jay

Ten dollars per hour. That's seventy dollars a week, which is two hundred and eighty dollars a month and that's over three thousand in one year. I am doing math in my head when I should be paying attention to what she is saying about Ollie. She needs to slow down. Shit. I think I missed something important but when she thrust the leash in my hand the frigging dog almost took off out the open door. *Jesus woman shut the door, it's freezing out there.*

She seems nervous. Maybe she thinks I am going to steal something. We went over all of that before, when I approached her about the job at the hospital. I heard her talking about needing someone to walk her dog and I wasn't about to let my opportunity to finally land a job pass. She asked me if I had references. By my puzzled expression, I think she got that I had no idea what she was talking about. My desperate look at the time might have helped. I did tell her she could call my school principal. Not sure she did, but a few days later she called me. So here I am, inside her designer house feeling like the unwanted flea.

I hear words like trial run, security cameras, a code for the back door and not much else. The frigging dog wants out. Know exactly how he feels.

He's now prancing, the click of his long nails driving me nuts while I watch him dance to his own beat. Poor sucker. Bet he sat in that stinky cage all day. Shit, he even pissed in it and by the way his body is twitching and moving I'm guessing he's got to go again.

The piece of paper she hands me with her cell number scrawled on it is my acceptance note. At the end of the week I'll get paid in cash. Suits me. Nodding, I say that's great. She tells me she will be gone when I am done walking Ollie, and that I have to put him back in his cage, and to make sure the door's locked. Guess he's got a knack for escaping.

One hour. Ten bucks. I am not going to screw this up.

She doesn't even know me and she's repeating that damn four digit security code, again. *Lady, I got it the first time*. Christ, what world does she live in? Certainly not mine. That was clear as Seven Up the minute I crossed the soccer field, moving from the welfare block of non-descript apartment buildings to single houses with lawns.

Middle-class, out of my league. This living room I stand in is as big as my entire apartment and there are two more levels and a big mother fucker of a garage I would kill to live in.

"Any problems, call me." She flings her large white purse over her shoulder, flicking her long blonde hair off her shoulders. She looks pretty in her nurse's uniform, but her eyes are red, like she's been crying.

"Thanks. I need to go now. Don't want to be late." Grabbing her coat, keys and purse, she ushers me and Ollie out the door, but there's a look on her face I can't quite figure out.

"I'll lock up, don't worry." Not sure why I feel the need to tell her the obvious but when she flashes a smile at me, I know those words were exactly what she needed to hear.

"Thanks, Jay. This means a lot." A slight pause fills the air but then Ollie barks, causing both of us to give shaky laughs. This job means more to me than her.

She climbs into her Escalade and quickly backs out of the driveway. I could have those hub caps off in six minutes flat. The minute she pulls out of the long driveway, I remember to lock up. My hands start to freeze. Tomorrow I'm wearing gloves. I'll have to swipe a pair from the school's lost and found box, but I don't care. Shit, it is freezing out.

I stuff a hand in my jeans trying to keep it warm when Ollie takes off. Jesus, she wasn't kidding. He pulls hard. Ollie is a boxer with sad brown eyes. They probably match my own. For a dog living in a fancy house I get the distinct impression he does not get the run of it.

My feet are flying along the icy sidewalk as I try to keep up with him. You'd have to be blind not to notice how all the driveways have been shoveled with the snow packed down around the sides like some freaking thing anal middle-class people do. The houses are a mix of brick and expensive siding and range from cranberry soda in color to chocolate bar brown. I feel like I'm a freaking foreigner in my own city. I don't recall ever stepping through the doors of one, besides to get my job. My face probably had that Disneyland look of awe plastered to it. Pathetic! The dog pulls me sharply to the left, forcing my feet to do double-time. I will be lucky if my arm doesn't get pulled out of its socket. Then I think about the money.

Seventy dollars. No, I got that wrong. She said she would pay me fifteen on the weekends because she knew I would be busy with extra-curricular activities. Her words, not mine. I didn't say anything when she spewed that nonsense. I do nothing on the weekend. Sad state of my life. That means in a year I will have close to four thousand dollars just from walking this dog.

Ollie pulls me sharply to the left, again toward the park the lady talked about. I almost land on my face, but honestly I don't care. Grinning ear to ear, my mind is thinking of all the important things I am going to buy with my money. Four thousand dollars rings in my head and I feel like I've finally won the lotto.

This is going to be the easiest one hour of my day. If I can keep my arm in my socket from the damn dog pulling me along the sidewalk like some scrambling wayward kite ready at any moment to plunge to the hard, unforgiving ground.

Heaven Is For Heroes

By P.J. Sharon

Excerpt

The sun sat low in the sky, an orange ball that promised another hot, steamy day ahead. I threw my towel onto a rock and kicked off my boots, the warm sand inviting under my toes. I shimmied out of my shorts and waded into the pond up to my thighs. A cold chill trickled up my spine. I thought of Alex for the millionth time in the last week, my heart taking another plunge into the depths of despair. I let out a frustrated groan. I hated being this out of control of my emotions. Maybe he had found closure in telling me to take a hike, but I didn't get to say what I wanted to say…should have said…needed to say. Instead I had pleaded like a pathetic, love sick little girl.

Angry with myself as much as I was Alex, I gave voice to my rage. "You stubborn, pig-headed, pain-in-the-ass…jerk!" I yelled to the leaves on the maple tree nearby. I felt stupid, but it was good to vent. A smidgeon of tension dropped from my shoulders. I did it again. "How could you be so selfish?" I shouted. "How could you walk away from the one person who knows you best…and still LOVES you…even though you are maddeningly stubborn and…and emotionally…immature!" I screamed. A flock of geese took flight off the surface of the still water.

I had to laugh at myself. Not because I was wrong, really, but because it was a terribly one-sided argument and I was acting a bit like an irrational shrew. It felt good not to have to hold back—constantly trying to be what Mom and Brig and…Alex…needed me to be.

I sank under the water up to my chin and felt the chill all the way to my bones, all of the heat I'd built up cooling instantly. I couldn't be mad at him. He was an honorable guy who thought he was doing the right thing by taking responsibility for a mistake. A part of me still couldn't believe it was Alex's fault. Where Levi was concerned, anything could have happened.

But the other part of me—the part that had worried about my brother and lied to protect him--knew that if Levi walked willingly to his death, my silence was the lie that made it possible. Maybe that was the truth I was trying to get to. I dunked under and came up slowly, dipping my head back and letting the water pour over me as if seeking some kind of baptism or forgiveness.

Pride's Run

By Cat Kalen

Excerpt

California Wine Country
August 23rd, six days until full moon

The click of the lock at the top of the stairwell is my only indication that morning is upon me. My ears perk up and I listen for the coming footfalls. The weight on the stairs combined with the creaking of each wooden step will let me know which handler has come for us this time, which unlucky puppet has drawn the short straw and is stuck with letting the dogs out, or in this case, the werewolves.

Sure, he'll come sauntering down the stairs sporting a brave face and looking at me with cold, dark eyes meant to intimidate. But the wolf inside me can smell his inner fear. Despite the fact that I'm the one caged, underneath the handler's cool, superficial shell he's the one who's truly afraid.

A long column of light filters down the stairs and I blink my eyes into focus as the bright rays infiltrate the pitch black cellar. I don't really need to blink. Not with my exceptional vision. But I do it anyway because sometimes I simply like to pretend I'm a normal seventeen-year-old girl, one who can't see in the dark. It's nonsense, I know. I'm not fooling anyone. Least of all myself.

The door yawns wider and before the first heavy boot, soiled with old blood that he'll pass off as wine stains, hits the top step, my senses go on high alert. I never know what morning will bring—or who will bring it.

A breeze rushes down the stairs ahead of the handler, carrying the aroma of the grand estate with it. I push past the metallic scent of dried blood to catch traces of grape juice in the air, a common smell on the majestic vineyard—that and illegal drugs, the estate's real source of income. Going beyond those familiar fragrances, I breathe deeper and get hints of fresh bread baking in the upstairs kitchen. It must be Thursday. Mica, the estate's cook, always bakes on Thursday.

In my human form I roll onto my side and lean toward the smell. Wistfully, my tongue darts out and brushes over my bottom lip. There is something about that scent that always entices me and before I can help it I envision myself eating a warm slice covered in rich creamy butter, crispy on the outside, moist and tender on the inside.

My nostrils widen, but I know the bread isn't meant for me and not even one delicious crumb will pass over my dry lips. Not unless Mica sneaks it to me. As much as I'd love to taste her offerings I don't like it when she takes chances for me. Disobedience is far too risky for the aging housekeeper. Despite that, my stomach growls in response to the aroma and I fight off the cravings. I can't hope for bread when it's unlikely that I'll even be given a scrap of food today, especially if I can't please him.

My master.

A boot hits the second step—the handlers always descend slowly—and as I stretch my legs out on my dusty mattress I hear the waking groans of Jace and Clover stirring in their own cages beside me. I glance their way, and that's when my attention falls on the one empty cage in the cellar. My mother's den. I breathe deep and fight off a pang of sadness that I cannot afford to feel.

I turn away from the empty cage and stare at the gray cement walls. I can't bear to look at her den any longer. It only reminds me of how they killed her and how all the pups were forced to watch—to learn that disobedience comes with a price. Guilt and sorrow eat at me to think that she'd died trying to free me.

When step number five creaks, I diligently try to shake off the memories. The handler is close which means I can't think about my mother right now. I push all thoughts of her aside, knowing that right now I have to think about my father and what he taught me before the master killed him. Never let them see your fear.

I harden myself.

Prepare.

Before my master's puppet even reaches the bottom step, I know it's the one they call Lawrence, the handler I hate the most. The one with a weak mind, strong back, teeth like baked beans and beady eyes that fit his ugly rat face.

He likes to call me kitten. I have a few choice names that I'd like to call him in return, but I always bite the inside of my cheek to resist the urge. Partly because I'd be whipped and partly because Miss Kara educated me and taught me all about manners. I realize that an educated wolf with manners might sound laughable. In my line of work, however, education and manners are as lethal as a bear trap to those I hunt. That's how I lure my marks, how I bait my prey. A pretty face and good grace go a long way for a trained killer like me.

My glance wanders to my leg, the one peeking out from beneath my ratty blanket, and my eyes are drawn to the long jagged scar tracking the length of my calf. I grimace. Even with my education and manners, I never forget what I really am. I'm never allowed to.

"Hey kitten," Lawrence says. Most would think the nickname is a play on my birth name, Pride. But I know it's the handler's way of cutting me down, to find control where he feels none. My parents called me Pride because I was their pride and joy. Lions live in a pride and since lions are cats…

He tosses a collar and chain into my cage. "Leash up."

I take note of the gun in his holster before my glance locks on his. As I give him a good hard stare, he flinches. The movement is slight, but I notice it. Dressed in my knee length nightgown, long hair loose around my shoulders, I might look like an average seventeen-year-old girl—harmless and innocent—but we all know I'm not.

Even though Lawrence keeps his face blank and stares down at me with those dark eyes of his, he reeks of terror. The scent is like a mixture of hot sweat and rotting compost. Oh, it's not pretty by any means. Nevertheless, the werewolf slumbering restlessly inside me feeds off his fear, thrives on it, so I inhale and draw it deep into my lungs.

Without taking my eyes off his, I take my time to leash up. My movements are slow and deliberate as I position the collar. Metal grinds metal and the sound cuts the silence as I secure it around my neck. The handler winces. So do the older, more obedient wolves that I bunk with.

Jace cuts me a glance, chocolate eyes now milky from old age warn me to behave. I realize he's doing it for my own good, but this morning I'm cold and hungry and in no mood for Lawrence's insults. Clover makes a noise to draw the handler's attention away from me, and all sets of eyes shift to her.

As Clover tries to pacify Lawrence, averting her gaze in a show of respect and making small talk about the weather, Lawrence opens my mother's former cage and pulls out her cot. He gives it a good hard shake and the breeze stirs the dust on the unfinished boards masquerading as our ceiling. The particles dance in the stairwell light before falling to the cold, cement floor.

When Lawrence tosses the cot into a corner I stiffen. It can only mean one thing. My mother has been gone for a little over a year now, and I know the master rarely keeps a cell empty for long, which makes me wonder when and how he's going to fill it?

Who will he breed?

I cringe at the thought of bringing puppies into this world, but know it's not something I have to worry about. The master would never breed a wolf like me. My mother always said I was a survivor, the only pup in a litter of three to make it, but hey, a runt is a runt. Thanks to Darwin and his theory of 'natural selection' a runt is a heritable trait that a pack can do without. When it comes to canine reproduction, only one motto dictates: runts need not apply.

Deep in the bowels of the estate's basement, the master keeps other wolves, separating the strong and young from one another. I'm smart enough to understand that he distances us so we can't conspire against him or speak telepathically. Wolves can only use telepathy when in animal form, however. Well, most wolves that is. Oddly enough, I along with Stone, an alpha wolf two years my senior, are able to communicate while in our human forms.

Sometimes the master does in-house breeding, sometimes he sends us out to one of his associates—other drug lords who also harbor werewolves. It's like he's running a regular old puppy mill in here. Except his puppies kill for him. Which begs the question, what does my master have in store for me today?